Baldwin on the Horizon

"Do you think we're supposed to carry our own things?" De asked.

"As if!" I scoffed. "There's got to be someone around here with, you know, one of those baggage racks on wheels."

"Cher!" De's mouth flopped open.

"What?" I asked. Shading my azure eyes with my hand, I squinted from the sun-drenched parking area into the ominously dark wilderness behind the entry arch.

"Is that a mirage or is there a Baldwin in flannel heading our way?" De asked.

"Hunk on the horizon," I confirmed.

Passing beneath the rustic arch of the spa, a monster hottie was striding toward us. His tanned face was lit by a full-out welcoming smile. Naturally sun-streaked sandy locks flopped fetchingly over his forehead, brushing the tops of his shades.

"Girlfriend, if that's what the concierge looks like, can you imagine the towel boys?" De murmured.

Other Clueless™ books

CLUELESS™
A novel by H. B. Gilmour
Based on the film written and directed by
Amy Heckerling

CLUELESS™: CHER'S GUIDE TO . . . WHATEVER
By H. B. Gilmour

CLUELESS™: ACHIEVING PERSONAL PERFECTION
By H. B. Gilmour

CLUELESS™: AN AMERICAN BETTY IN PARIS
By Randi Reisfeld

CLUELESS™: CHER NEGOTIATES NEW YORK
By Jennifer Baker

CLUELESS™: CHER'S FURIOUSLY FIT WORKOUT
By Randi Reisfeld

Available from ARCHWAY Paperbacks

CLUELESS™

Friend or Faux

H.B. Gilmour

AN ARCHWAY PAPERBACK
Published by POCKET BOOKS
New York London Toronto Sydney Tokyo Singapore

AN ARCHWAY PAPERBACK *Original*

An Archway Paperback published by
POCKET BOOKS, a division of Simon & Schuster Inc.
1230 Avenue of the Americas, New York, NY 10020

™ and Copyright © 1996 by Paramount Pictures

ISBN: 0-671-00323-2

First Archway Paperback printing November 1996

10 9 8 7 6 5 4 3 2 1

AN ARCHWAY PAPERBACK and colophon are registered trademarks of Simon & Schuster Inc.

Printed in the U.S.A.

IL: 7+

To Jessi, as always, with love

Chapter 1

Which one should I pack, the Todd Oldham tile print or the Mizrahi silk halter top?" I asked my best friend, Dionne.

We were hangin' in my room, which was originally decorated by this exalted New York designer and redone by a major West Coast consultant. It's got a Laura-Ashley-goes-Malibu kind of ambience, feminine yet expensive.

"Hello, we are going to experience nature, Cher," Dionne reminded me. "Not valet parking."

De was peering over my shoulder. Her salon dreads were like brushing against my own freshly highlighted blond hair. We were both staring at my computer screen.

My entire wardrobe, which is one of the total foundations of my life, is programmed into my PC and coded by color, season, activity, and designer. There are those, like my envious friend Amber, who find this obsessive. Well, excuse me for needing order in my life. Some people are comfortable with chaos. I am so not one of them.

"Girlfriend," I responded, "the flyer Ms. Stoeger gave us said a graduation ceremony was part of the package. Are we like going to grasp our diplomas in casual wear? Do our acceptance speeches in leotards and sweats? Don't tell me you didn't pack a single festive ensemble."

"What was I thinking?" Dionne lamented.

It was the night before one of the most eagerly anticipated initiation rites of our young lives. De and I were departing at dawn for our first spa encounter! And we owed it all to Ms. Stoeger, the wonder-jock.

Okay, pop quiz. Your gym teacher offers you a three-day total fitness package in the way pastoral Santa Monica Mountains, cuisine and accommodations included—or two grueling weeks of phys ed as usual. Doy, guess which one we selected—like, in a heartbeat?

I and Dionne could hardly believe it. Yet one day in PE, our teacher, Ms. Stoeger, handed out this page describing a program called the Beverly Hills Nature Experience. And according to Stoeger, whoever signed on for the program and graduated from it got to legally blow off PE for two entire weeks. Oh, no. What a brutal choice.

A popular package, as you might imagine, the Beverly Hills Nature Experience was fully booked for weekends. So high school students could use "the verdant facilities" only during the week. Which meant that if you signed up you would have to miss three whole days of classes.

De and I were all, Yes! And I have to say, my teachers were fully golden. Way supportive. Not one of them objected to my going.

I phoned De on my way out of Mr. Hall's class. "He signed my permission slip," I informed her, receiving the usual waves and whistles of my classmates as I moved through the halls of Bronson Alcott High. De and I are furiously popular, which is way fun—except when you're in a hurry and have to like stop every two seconds to acknowledge an accolade or return a smile. Then, being sought-after is like a total curse. "His was the last signature I needed," I said, all excited. "We're on our way. Isn't Hall just the bomb?"

"Truly decent, though short and bald," De agreed. "Meet you in the Quad in two minutes."

I shook my hair à la Cindy doing her Revlon thing, and my lustrous blond strands, alive with color, shimmered and bounced. "Where are you now?" I asked De, then mouthed a silent "thank you" to Alana, who'd said in passing that my highlights looked choice.

"I'm leaving algebra," De said. "Just stepping out the door."

I acknowledged Sean's wink, Lorenzo's smile, and Amber's predictably sullen glare. "Hanratty's room?" I said. "I'm there."

Dionne and I practically ran into each other in the corridor. "Did Hanratty sign your permission slip?" I inquired, clicking off my mobile.

"Is an isosceles triangle unilateral?" she asked, tucking her phone into her petite Coach purse.

"Like, no, it's not."

"Well, anyway, Ms. Hanratty did sign. She was my last signature!" We gave each other a limp-wristed high-five.

"How excellent is it that we are out of here for three magnifico days?" I said as we headed for the food court to do lunch. I pulled out my cellular again and gave Brent a jingle. "Hey, Brent, Cher Horowitz here. We'll be two for lunch at our regular table in a few minutes, okay? Yeah? Thanks. Peace." I clicked off.

"Okay, we're reserved," I told De. "Brent says Tai is waiting for us, and Summer and Janet. Oh, I forgot to tell you. You know where it said in the flyer 'verdant facilities'? Well, Janet Hong says *verdant* refers to vegetation. Which probably means vegetarian cuisine," I enthused. "We'll shed beaucoup pounds! And there's probably a hot tub in every cabin."

"And peppermint oil massages?" De's gorgeous hazel eyes went all misty in expectation.

"And fabulous freebies," I ventured, "like you get at charity benefit galas. You know, those miniature shopping bags stuffed with manufacturers' samples of outdoorsy products and SPF moisturizers and other protective cosmetics."

Jesse Fiegenhut approached us, carrying a carton of CDs. "My dad got these promo copies of this radical new group," he said, handing each of us a disk. "They're called Cyberscuz."

Jesse, like Dionne's boyfriend, Murray, is a member of the Crew, an informal assemblage of Bronson Alcott's premiere hotties of the male persuasion. If you're into high school boys, which I am rarely, the Crew is like an acceptable pool to draw from. They understand attire, they throw the most excellent fies-

4

tas, their families are furiously well-off, and they're like most extremely attractive. Jesse himself has dark, wavy hair and a bod of Baldwinian potential.

"Cyberscuz?" Dionne repeated.

The CD art showed an ethnically diverse crew, all but one of them sporting wispy slacker chin hairs.

"They're a frantic new sound," Jesse assured us. "It's like Hootie meets the Cranberries, only their lead vocalist is practically a Madonna clone." Which explained why her chin was clean, I supposed.

Jesse totally idolized the Material Girl. He owned multiple CD copies of her entire oeuvre.

"Thanks, Jesse," I said, slipping the disk into my bag, although I am so overstocked in the CD area. "You're joining us for lunch, of course?"

"Why is this day different from all other days?" he said, and De and I waggled our fingers at him and continued across the Quad.

As we approached our outdoor table, which was shaded by a stand of palm trees surrounded by a bright floral border of hibiscus and impatiens, we heard a familiar greeting: "Yo, yo, wassup, Cher? Dionne, where you been? I been beepin' you, woman."

"Hi, Murray," I said, stepping out of the way so that he and De could perform their ritual dialogue for the gathering student body. Kids come from all over the campus to hear Dionne and Murray's disputes.

De did a whimper of frustration and shook her gorgeous head. Then I—and every other youthful spectator—silently mouthed the traditional opening line along with her: "Don't call me woman!"

Black knit cap pulled low on his brow, Murray stared at her through small, round Oliver Peoples shades.

Then he unzipped his oversize Nautica canvas jacket and hiked up one leg of his patriotic, flannel-lined Hilfiger sweatpants, exposing a muscular brown calf. His Calvin socks drooped over his glove-leather Timberland high tops.

"Word up." Murray flashed De a dazzling smile. Sunlight danced off the braces that accessorized his teeth. "What you doggin' about now? You be disrespectin' me, woman."

Murray believes that street argot is a totally valid form of self-expression. Dionne—whose mom is a major publicist and behind-the-scenes Hollywood player whose Rolodex is insured for about a gazillion dollars by Lloyds of London—so does not agree.

They argue about it all the time, primarily in public places. They're both excellent debaters. And they've got extremely committed fans.

"I'm Audi, De," I said. "I'm like totally starving. But we have to talk soon so that we can plan our spa wardrobe. I hate waiting till the last minute."

De broke off her bitter remarks to Murray long enough to throw a kiss my way. "Me, too," she assured me with a radiant smile.

Now here it was—the last minute. We were leaving in the early A.M. for the Beverly Hills Nature Experience, and I was still at the keyboard, pondering ensembles.

"So, are you packing your hot rollers?" De asked, abandoning me as I accessed footwear.

"I guess, if you're not," I said. "But you won't need hot rollers with dreads, will you?"

"I'm thinking of having extensions done instead."

She threw herself down on the cushioned wicker chaise longue next to my king-size bed—both done in contrasting Ashley florals.

I was shocked. I turned from the computer. "Dionne, it's like nearly eight o'clock at night. We are Audi in mere hours. How are you going to trade your dreads for extensions before morning?"

"Excuse me? Like Sergio doesn't make house calls? When Carolina went to the Awards, he blow-dried her in the limo." Carolina is De's mom. "This is an important event, Cher. You were right, we should look our very best. So, when I go home tonight, I'm going to throw my silk clutch coat by Donna Karan into the Vuitton steamer, and then I'll call Sergio, and—"

"Dionne, you're bringing a steamer trunk?"

"Yes. I mean we're traveling light, right?" She aimed a French nail at the large suitcases rapidly filling on my bed. It was true, there were only two of them.

"Two pieces of luggage for three days *is* a risk, but I'm prepared to rough it. Of course, I haven't packed cosmetics yet," I hedged, shutting down the computer.

"So what did you decide?" De asked. "The Oldham or the Mizrahi?"

"For the graduation ceremony? I think the red Azzedine Alaïa with black feathered trim. It's lively without being ostentatious, and the feathers are a nice environmental touch. You know what's the best part about this trip?" I said.

"That we get to spend three fabulous days away from school, and when we come back, we don't have to do phys ed again for two whole weeks!"

"And it's like a total no-brainer," I enthused. "It'll be the easiest three days of our young and excellent lives.

I mean, just look at this flyer." I carried the piece of paper Stoeger had given us over to the chaise and smoothed it out. "Here's the strategic sentence," I said, pointing to "The Beverly Hills Nature Experience is a challenging survival adventure to help teens develop confidence and self-esteem."

"If we just diagram that sentence, Dionne, it becomes obvious that we've already aced the course! Look. Take 'self-esteem,'" I said. "We are like totally fraught with it."

"Abundantly," De agreed. "We have furiously thriving self-esteem."

"Which we have absolutely worked for," I pointed out. "Consider the time, energy, and plastic we've allocated to self-improvement. Every compliment we get . . ."

"Every wannabe strolling the Quad in an accessory or hairstyle that we have personally pioneered . . ." said De.

"Every shred of admiration and envy that's come our way, we have so earned."

"Oh, and then there's 'confidence,'" Dionne continued, warming to the exercise.

"Ours is unassailable," I stated. "Do we not believe in ourselves to the max? Is insecurity even an issue—ever?"

De bit her lip and, to my astonishment, seemed actually to be thinking it over. "I once had to ask Carolina about whether green made my skin look sallow," she confessed at last.

"Duh, that's style, not insecurity. And finally we come to 'a challenging survival experience.'"

"'Survival'?" De repeated. "Cher, we are popular, beautiful, and smart."

"Face it, girlfriend, we are *so* beyond survival."

De got up and smacked me a limp high-five. We were jumping around, shrieking, "We already aced the course, we aced the course!" when the phone rang.

I hit the speaker button and said, "Bueno?"

Tai's innocent voice crackled through the off-white console. "So, are you guys totally psyched or what?"

"Yes!" De shouted. I gave her a look. "But we're really going to miss you," she amended sympathetically.

Tai's mother, as well as four out of six of her teachers, had refused to sign her permission slip. Although Dionne and I tutored her to the best of our abilities, Tai was skidding toward permanent study-hall status.

"Well, at least I'm not the only one not going," she said bravely. "Janet Hong's allergic to wheat grass. Summer has to attend a bat mitzvah. And Amber got a note from her cosmetic surgeon saying she couldn't engage in physical activity until her scars healed."

De rolled her eyes. "What did she have fixed this time?"

"She said chin implants, but I don't believe her," Tai ventured. "I think it's just 'cause it's Italian Fashion Week on CNN and she wants to stay home to watch Elsa Klensch."

"I'm taping it," I said.

"Listen, you guys. Have a great time, okay?" Tai was all melancholy. "Um, Ryder's here, too. He says like, 'Hi.'"

Ryder Hubbard is Tai's latest crush. He's a wickedly nimble in-line skater who's taken one too many falls.

Two minutes after we hung up, Daddy knocked on my door. My dad is a brilliant and famous attorney. His vicious courtroom tactics are furiously admired; he's like this cross between Oliver Wendell Holmes and a pit bull. I pick out all his clothes. Daddy dresses wonderfully. Which is very important for attorneys today because of all the media attention they get. Court TV has been after him for years, but he wouldn't even make a cameo appearance on their show because they pay so badly.

"Remember, Cher," Daddy said, "and you, too, Dionne. Don't sign anything when you get to this place without faxing it to me first. No releases, no waivers."

"Daddy, you know we wouldn't," I said, "but it's totally safe."

"It's probably just like Rancho Mirage or the Golden Door," De tried to reassure him.

"It had better be or you, Cher, are taking back every single outfit you bought for this little trip!"

I gasped and instinctively clutched the new silk lingerie bag I'd gotten practically for free after a major cosmetics purchase at the Dior counter at Nordstrom.

"Even if it's the best spa in the world, things happen. I had a client who slid off a massage table during a hot-oil treatment at one of those places," Daddy reminisced fondly. "And one with a face-lift whose staples popped during a yoga class." He shook his head gravely. "I don't want anything bad happening to you two."

"Oh, Daddy, you are brutally sweet to be concerned," I said, beaming at him. "But Dionne and I are like way prepared. I've packed total sun block, protein hair conditioner with aloe vera *and* vitamin E, a mild hydra-balance nonsoap cleansing complex with purifying botanicals and herbal extracts, Blistex, Advil—"

"And don't forget," De broke in, "this trip is sponsored by our school, which is like way conservative and frantically strict. Like if you don't return your library book on time, the fine is deducted directly from your annuity fund. And next semester they're placing a limit on on-campus cash machine withdrawals."

I gave Daddy a big kiss. "Don't worry," I said. "I mean, what could happen to us anyway? We are about to embark on a first-class, fun-filled, vegetarian wilderness adventure. It's like totally luxurious and safe."

Chapter 2

Not even!

The next day De and I climbed into the stretch limo Daddy had leased for our journey, clinked Perrier bottles, and kicked back for the trip.

One minute we were cruising up this fully scenic route that was all *Lifestyles of the Rich and Famous*, only in earth tones. Everybody you'd ever heard of had a serious casa or villa or rancho off this winding canyon road. There were known celebrities all over the place— literally. We passed them doing laps in the rosy morning light.

"I swear that was Meryl Streep jogging with Clint Eastwood," De said as our car spewed dust at a handsome older couple trotting along the roadside.

"I can't tell," I said, looking out the rear window.

"They're like doubled over coughing. I think Clint needs EMS."

Then, like a minute later, the elegant residences disappeared. Pruned shrubbery gave way to wild palms and thorny underbrush with spiky cactus poking up here and there. The wide paved road went viciously rural, as if someone had run out of cash or cement, and we were bumping along a treacherous rock-strewn path.

"Where are we?" De held on to the bright vinyl hat that matched the adorable yellow micromini she was wearing. Her eyes were wild with fear.

"I don't know," I confessed, "but I wish I had the local Range Rover dealership." I had chosen a hot red tube dress for traveling. And though I had been fully briefed on the rustic aspect of our trip, I couldn't resist slipping into a pair of high-heeled faux lizard strap sandals.

"Cher, this can't be the right way."

"Excuse me, Hal." I rapped on the driver's partition. "Are we lost?"

"Al," he corrected me. "And I don't think so."

"There must be some mistake," De insisted. "I mean, I know nature. This isn't nature. This is like an abandoned lot in East L.A., only without the plastic flowers."

We hardly had time to adjust to the savage vista. Our chauffeur spun a wheelie into a dirt parking area, slammed on the brakes, and said, "This is it."

I could not believe my eyes. "Dionne," I said, "there is not one other limousine in this entire lot."

"Hello," said De. "Do you even see a Porsche or a Beemer or an Alfa on the premises?"

We were surrounded by buses.

"Who are these people?" De asked as adolescent after ill-clad adolescent straggled off the buses. They were shouldering knapsacks and duffel bags—serious knapsacks, not like your cute stuffed-animal-shaped backpacks or even the tawdry everyday canvas you can get at the Gap. These had metal parts, utensils hanging off them, and must've weighed forty pounds apiece. They looked like they'd been snagged off Sherpa guides in Tibet.

We were way disappointed.

"Dionne, I'm sure we can clear this up in no time," I said supportively. "We'll just wait for the concierge to help us with our luggage, and then I'll have a little chat with whoever's in charge."

A thorough professional, Al popped the trunk of our dust-defiled burgundy stretch and hauled out our luggage. He piled my glove-leather Ralph Lauren safari suitcases and spacious vinyl cosmetic kit on top of Dionne's Louis Vuitton trunk, then gently laid across them the hanging bags we'd brought for formal wear. When all our things were stacked in the dirt, he presented the car voucher for me to sign.

"Cher, maybe we ought to reconsider," De suggested.

"And do like what, two weeks of arduous calisthenics in Stoeger's class? Girlfriend, you can't judge a spa by its parking lot. The rest of the facilities are probably fully four-star! Anyway, De, like the brochure said, it's an adventure."

"I believe the exact phrase was 'survival adventure'," De reminded me.

With a frisson of misgiving, I watched our limo depart, a farewell wall of dust lingering in its wake.

I looked around the heinous parking lot and the dark rustic terrain surrounding it. "I guess we're not in Kansas anymore," I said.

"What does that mean?" De asked.

"It's like when things turn out differently from what you expect. You know, it's from *The Wizard of Oz*. It's what Dorothy says when she wakes up in this bitterly alien yet colorful world."

"Your point being?" De wanted to know.

"Well, everything worked out for her in the movie. Although first she had to like flee these majorly disgusting monkeys."

Well, I cannot tell you how long De and I cooled our Chanel Boutique sabrina-heel pumps and Gucci faux lizard sandals respectively, waiting for someone to help with our luggage. The bus people had schlepped the last of their forestry gear through the woodsy archway into the Beverly Hills Nature Experience. The buses were gone. The only signs of life in the parking area, besides us, were three generic domestic vehicles—like a Dart and a Pinto, I think—and whatever was rattling through the trash bin on the far side of the lot.

"Do you think we're supposed to carry our own things?" De asked.

"As if!" I scoffed. "There's got to be someone around here with, you know, one of those baggage racks on wheels. At this point, I'm not even expecting a uniform or anything. A human being with an oxcart would do."

"Cher!" De's mouth flopped open.

"What?" I asked. Shading my azure eyes with my hand, I squinted from the sun-drenched parking area into the ominously dark wilderness behind the entry arch.

"Is that a mirage or is there a Baldwin in flannel heading our way?" De asked.

"Hunk on the horizon," I confirmed.

Passing beneath the rustic arch of the spa, a monster hottie was striding toward us. His tanned face was lit by a full-out welcoming smile. Naturally sun-streaked sandy locks flopped fetchingly over his fore-head, brushing the tops of his shades.

"Girlfriend, if that's what the concierge looks like, can you imagine the towel boys?" De murmured.

Okay, so his sunshades were your generic off-the-rack, no-designated-designer type. But they looked good on him—and even better off, when his dewy dark eyes started scoping us.

"Hi, I'm Ian," he said in this mellow baritone. As if to prove it, he indicated the nametag pinned to his classic flannel plaid. The plastic-protected sticker on his chest said: IAN. BHNE.

Dionne threw him a radiant dental greeting. "What an interesting name. Is that like Yugoslavian or some-thing?" she asked.

I rolled my eyes and said pointedly, "Doy, BHNE stands for Beverly Hills Nature Experience."

She got all defensive. "It could have been one of those vowel-less Eastern European names that are way difficult to pronounce," she insisted. "You never know."

"Actually, it's Ian Mallory," the hottie explained.

"I'm Cher," I said, flipping back my long, formerly

squeaky-clean hair. "And this is my best friend, Dionne. We're with the Bronson Alcott group. And we've been like broiling out here, waiting for someone to help us with all this." I waved at the stack of luggage growing dusty behind me.

"Bronson Alcott High School, sure. Most of your friends arrived a couple of hours ago. They're settling in now."

"Look, you can't possibly carry all this without wheels," I added. "So we can probably handle one hanger bag between us, right, De?"

"I think so," she said. "My trainer is very pro-lifting, and I don't need a weight belt for under five pounds. Plus I've got nail glue in my cosmetic case."

"No problem," Ian said, loading up. "I'm one of the BHNE nature guides, but I'd be glad to help you."

As we stumbled behind him over root and rock, De and I tried to acquire major stats on Ian.

"How long have you been into nature and all?" De asked, hoping to zone in on his age.

"Ever since I was a kid. My family had a cabin in Idaho, where we'd hang out summers——"

"So you were a kid," De interrupted tactfully. "Like how long ago would you say that was?"

Ian laughed. "I'll be twenty next fall."

Picking my way between pebbles and twigs, I said, "And this is your chosen career path?" I didn't mean to sound all judgmental. But the open toes of my sandals were rapidly filling with sharp environmental objects, a painful reminder that style has its price. I couldn't wait to change into my brand-new spectator mules by Cole-Haan.

"I'm an architecture student," Ian said, holding

back a low tree branch with his broad, flanneled shoulders so that De and I could continue on without lacerations. "I'm working my way through school doing carpentry and odd jobs like this one."

"Way cool," I said, courteously using an older term. "I think architects are so . . . constructive. And brutally choice."

"Cher! Look!" Dionne gasped in horror and stopped so suddenly that I crashed into her. Only my palms against the back of her cap-sleeve shantung blouse kept me from falling.

We had emerged from the wilderness onto the set of *Deliverance*. I mean the only thing missing from the sagging cabin before us was a couple of genetically impaired banjo players rocking on the porch.

"Excuse me," I said as Ian set down our luggage. "There must be some mistake."

"It's not much to look at, is it?" he concurred. "But it's just as comfortable as the other cabins. The ones nearer the lake filled up fast. You two are our last arrivals. At least you'll have privacy here. You'll be rooming alone."

"Are there at least two double beds in there?" De asked skeptically.

Ian laughed again and shook his head no. Dionne brightened suddenly. "How fun. They're king-size, right?"

"Hello, where is the hot tub?" I asked. "That teeny-tiny closetlike structure built onto the side of this hut cannot possibly house a full-size hot tub or even a decent sauna."

"No," Ian said, "that's your latrine."

"Latrine? As in . . . bathroom? That's our *bath-room?*" I gasped.

De screamed.

I grabbed her hand. "Be brave," I whispered. "Let's look inside."

"I don't care if we're not in Kansas anymore," De whimpered. "But, Cher, this isn't even the United States!"

Chapter 3

*W*hen Dionne and I got up the nerve to venture into our cabin—or the Crypt, as we shortly began to call it—the first thing we noticed was the damp darkness and the creaking floor. The smell didn't hit us until a second later. It was bitterly aromatic: a blast of skunk spray, a soupçon of droppings, a tart musk of mildew. Your basic Eau de Woodland.

The anorexic bungalow had not two, but *eight* beds stuffed into it. "Let's see," I said, desperately trying to make De laugh. "That's Sleepy, Bashful, Happy, and Doc— Sorry, Dionne. Looks like you'll have to sleep in the woods."

She was so not amused.

Needless to say, none of the beds was king, queen, or double. They were slender steel affairs, with thin striped mattresses rolled up on them. Your basic jail surplus. The closet was a jump rope strung across one end of the place. The dresser was a series of cob-webbed cubbyholes about the size of shoe boxes. The only way out of this shanty was a lopsided screen door that screeched at the slightest touch.

And those were the luxury items.

What was *not* there was a toilet, sink, or shower. There was no running water, no electricity, no mirror, no outlet for blow-dryers or hot rollers; not even the most basic necessities for skin, nail, and hair care.

We could not believe we'd been assigned such shoddy accommodations.

De was close to tears. "I don't understand why my mother goes to places like this," she wailed. "This must be the total skid row of spas!"

I grabbed De's hand and we marched out onto the porch. "I demand to see the person in charge!" I shouted into the wilderness.

Serious mistake.

My furious cry resounded through the forest. Before the last echo died away, there was a bleakly ferocious thrashing in the bushes. Some enormous animal must have been hunting there and, bugging at my shout, was about to leap out—possibly with a baby gazelle in its teeth—to destroy us.

De and I grabbed each other and stood quaking on the already shaky porch.

What emerged, with a whistle gleaming on its chest and a clipboard grasped in its stocky hand, was what could have been the original model from which all the Ms. Stoegers in the world had been carved.

"I am Allison Richard," the awesome creature thundered. "I'm in charge here. And who are you two?"

"Did she say 'Rigid'?" De whispered.

"If she didn't, she'd be wrong." I cleared my throat and stepped forward. My heel went through the deck, somewhat spoiling the moment.

"I am Cher Horowitz," I said, pulling my shoe up through the rotting wood. "You've probably heard of my father, the pit bull of the appellate court. He's a totally ferocious attorney. And let me tell you, whoever you are, that this little-house-on-the-prairie setup you've got here is just a lawsuit waiting to happen."

"Really?" The troll in bushwear and shades cocked her head at us. A cruel smile dented her stony face. "And you are?" She turned to De.

"I'm Dionne," De announced, stepping forward. "So you're what, like the CEO here?"

The khaki-clad tower of power whipped off her supermarket eyewear. "I'm in charge of you girls," she hissed.

De shuddered. But I couldn't help noticing that Allison's eyes were surprisingly attractive. Dark and doe-shaped but woefully underplayed. A decent lash thickener would have done wonders for her. But then so would a couple of months off carbos.

"Er, so does that mean Ian is like in charge of the boys?" De asked.

"Boys?" Allison's sneer would have made Ms. Stoeger proud. "There are no boys here. Ian Mallory is our white-water rafting expert. And then there's Oscar Epstein, whom you'll also meet. Oscar is the author of two seminal works on foraging."

"'Foraging'?" said De.

Allison nodded curtly. "You two are late and I'm very busy. I'll have someone drop off your blankets, bed linens, and other provisions. Get settled, then come find me. I'm the third cabin from the lake." Then she marched back into the underbrush.

"We are so Audi," De said, reaching for her cellular.

"Not even!" I gripped her hands, gently restraining her. "Are you postal, girlfriend? I'm not returning two suitcases' worth of golden goodies just because this venue isn't up to prime spa standards. Remember, Daddy said I'd have to bring back everything I bought."

"Forgive me," she said.

We sat on the front steps of the porch for a couple of minutes in mute dejection. Which I totally hate. Downcast is so not my thing. Neither is quitting.

"De," I said, leaping up, but cautiously. I only had so many pairs of shoes to destroy. "If you've got a lemon, make lemonade!"

"Hello! If I had a lemon, I'd eat it," she retorted. "Cher, I am brutally depressed and totally famished."

"That is so textbook," I said encouragingly. "I read in *Sassy* that lots of despondent people have eating disorders. Girlfriend, the best natural antidepressant is physical activity. Come on, De, let's break out the brooms and make something of this hovel."

"What, like a clean hovel?" she offered.

I pulled her to her feet. Reluctantly, she followed me back into the dank room, which I was now determined to transform.

We unpacked and changed into casual wear. I chose

bold tangerine polyurethane jeans with a simple cotton tank top by Jil Sander. "So, survey says on Allison Richard?" I asked.

"Safari garb by J C Penney—and I do not mean their Cheryl Tiegs signature collection," De said, wriggling into a nylon-Lycra striped shirt and five-pocket stretch pants by Guess?.

"Too much Häagen-Dazs, too little Buns of Steel," she continued. "Survey says: Richard is a major home-improvement candidate, requiring a radical Susan Powter–level renovation."

Although it was a borderline call, I opted for Reebok cross-trainers over my T-strap wedge shoes from Stephane Kelian.

"She's got great eyes," I mused aloud. "And her skin is way healthy."

"Yes, and there's so much of it," De said. "Cher, you're not thinking makeover, are you?"

"At the moment, it's just an intriguing possibility. We'll see." I shrugged. "Right now, this"—I indicated the seriously dilapidated interior of our cabin—"is a vicious priority."

Using the supplies delivered to our squeaky screen door while we were changing, we did a minor tidy on the Crypt.

Making the beds was a problem. Which to select? De and I bounced on all eight. I felt the best choices were the only two that didn't give way under us. We hauled the broken beds outside, but kept the mattresses. Four piled up apiece made a moderately comfortable bed. A little high off the ground, but at least you couldn't feel steel ribs sticking in your back.

The sheets and pillowcases were like maybe a ten

thread count. They had the scratchy consistency of cheap paper towels, but they were clean. The blankets were army issue, probably from a cavalry unit. Possibly used by the horses themselves.

I have to say we worked wonders with limited resources. Cleaning utensils consisted of a dustpan and broom. And then we got wooden matches, basic white candles, and an oil lamp each. But we were fully innovative.

My suitcases made excellent end tables. We artfully tossed reading material on top of them: *YM, People, Vogue.* We threw a huge shawl over De's trunk, placed my three-way cosmetic mirror on top of it, and set candles on either side of the mirror. It was like this makeup altar. We sprinkled sachet beads and fragrant bath grains into every musty nook and cranny. And spritzed Chanel, cK, and Shalimar all over the place.

After all that domestic activity, De was too exhausted to be blue, but she was still ferociously hungry. I was also having cravings of the culinary kind. So we moseyed toward the sound of burbling water, to the cabin of She-Ra, Wearer of the Whistle.

Allison was standing outside a rustic sty not unlike our own. "You're just in time," she called to us over the heads of the girls gathered around her. Among them were Summer, Ariel, Alana, and Baez.

They shrieked when they saw us emerging from the wilderness.

"Cher! De!" We slapped high-fives and went, "Do you believe this place? Is this like Spa by Wal-Mart? Did you even see a sauna anywhere?" The whistle shrilled us to silence.

"All right then." Allison continued the speech she'd

been giving before we showed up. "I think some of you may have had the wrong idea of what the Beverly Hills Nature Experience is all about." She threw a significant look in our direction. "Our purpose is not to pamper or please you—"

"How contemporary," Alana remarked, rolling her eyes.

"Give me news, not history," I agreed.

"But to teach you how to survive in the wilderness, to introduce you to basic skills—"

De raised her hand. "Excuse me, Ms. Richard?"

"That's okay. Call me Allison, we're informal here."

Informal? Allison was wearing a wrinkled yet durable khaki shirt that in a crunch could be recycled as a tent. Her scruffy boots and camouflage pants were the kind of garb you'd see on like the Militia Home Shopping Network.

Informal was a grievous understatement, I thought, but De just said, "Okay, well, Allison, speaking of survival, like when do we eat?"

"Good question, Dionne," said our guide. "I was just going to talk about foraging. Does anyone here know what the word 'forage' means?"

It was like a complete doy-fest; a shrugging, head-shaking epidemic. Then Summer went, "Allison, Allison!" She was waving her hand. "It's like cereal, right? Like wasn't that what Goldilocks ate, you know, *chez trois* bears?"

Everyone snickered and giggled but Summer and Allison.

"No, isn't it? Come on," Summer kept saying. "It is."

Allison's mouth fell open. She cleared her throat.

"Well, it *does* have something to do with food," she finally admitted. "To forage is to look for and gather food. So, to answer Dionne's question, you eat as soon as you find, catch, and cook your food."

I focused in on the word "find"—envisioning a scavenger hunt for veggie burgers.

"Catch?" De whispered to me. "Excuse me, Allison," she said. "What are we talking about here, like throwing food around and catching it? Or catch as in run after a chicken?"

"Eeeww! Gross." Everyone shuddered and gagged.

"Cook?" said Baez. "I don't cook. Nella, our chef, cooks. Once my mother cooked. But I don't cook."

There were grumbles of agreement. A nasty mood was building. I tried to head it off.

"Allie, listen, I've got my cell phone right here and abundant plastic. We can order in."

Everyone was all, Yes!

Almost everyone.

Allison blew her whistle. It was bitterly piercing and totally deflated the solution-oriented positive energy I'd managed to create.

"People! Attention!" she shouted. "We are discussing foraging. Foraging is a basic survival skill—"

"Hello! Like having a cellular isn't?" Alana demanded.

She was viciously ignored. Allison rolled on like a Laguna Beach mudslide. "And so is fishing. You'll learn how to fish: how to catch, identify, clean, and fillet your own fish—"

"As if!" I told De. "Like what is this spa supposed to be teaching us to survive as—sushi chefs?"

The group was divided in its response. Some were

relieved to know they were going fishing and didn't have to bring down their own lamb chops with a bow and arrow. Others were squeamish but willing.

"The fishing group will work with Ian," Allison continued. "And some of you will go into the woods with Oscar to pick edible wild berries, nuts, and greens. The rest will help me prepare a campfire site. Most of you met Ian and Oscar when you arrived. Oscar's right up there—"

De and I followed Allie's pencil point to a stand of fir trees near her cabin. The winner of the Woody Allen look-alike contest was leaning against a tree, reading.

"He majorly looks like an Oscar," I noted.

"As if I!" Summer broke in. "I mean, did you guys even watch the Awards?"

"Hello—we're not talking 'May I have the envelope, please,'" De informed her.

I saw Ian down at the lake. He was all busy and attractive, fiddling with some generic fishing poles. He looked up, caught me scoping him, and gave me a big smiley wave—which I rampantly returned.

Aside from his being a full-out Baldwin, Ian had mentioned that he did carpentry.

I'd had a vision when De and I were cleaning our bungalow. I could see the place shaping up as an adorable rustic retreat. I had the concept, but not the skill or tools. So there were a few things I thought Ian might do around our cabin. For an architecture student, they'd be way enriching. I felt I could offer him both a challenge and a choice opportunity for self-expression.

"De, let's try it," I decided. "Daddy loves fishing. It can't be all that bad. I mean, we don't really have to eat what we catch. Although if you have to include fat grams in your diet, fish fat is fully golden, like almost negative calories."

De looked lakeward and gave Ian a little wave. "What if we get put into the nut-gathering group?" she asked. "Or have to what, chop down trees? Cher, I just had acrylics repaired."

"Leave it to me," I said, turning to study Allison Richard. She was checking stuff on her clipboard, clearly trying to figure out who the lucky fishers would be and who would get to risk Lyme disease with Oscar.

Her choppy, not totally unattractive hair fell over her glasses, which she kept hiking up her pert nose. That nose was an oasis of potential in a desert of flesh. Of the several pounds Allison could lose, two were in her cheeks.

Three steps below Allison, a dozen girls were grumbling among themselves, bitterly restless and discontented. In addition to no hot tubs or ambience, there was an appalling lack of leadership here.

"At this point, I'll do anything to eat," De said. "I can't believe I didn't pack a single snack. I was so looking forward to a healthful regimen. Now, I'm all like, sell my phone for a Frozfruit."

"You?" Ariel said. "I'm sorry I didn't pack my dad's Ensure."

I eyed Big Al again. She was deeply oblivious, still communing with her clipboard.

I raised my hands above my head. "Hello. Hello, people," I said.

Everyone turned my way. "So who loved *The Sound of Music?*" I asked. "Remember when they were like all skipping and singing in the meadow?"

A few hands went up.

"Okay, you, you, you, and Summer—you'll be the foragers. There's a great meadow out there, and somebody's got to pick it."

Allison looked up.

"What are you doing?" she demanded.

"Allie, look, any resemblance between this place and the Beverly Hills we know and shop is strictly imaginary. Face it," I said, cutting through the crowd to join her on the porch. "Aside from taking the name of my community in vain and grievously misrepresenting it, you've got other problems."

I counted them off on my fingers. "The cabins are whack. There's no buffet. Amenities are at a low ebb. And your expectations are way out of line. We are tired, hungry, irritable . . . disappointed is an extreme understatement. Plus many of us have brutally influential parents. You've taken on much too much responsibility here. The way I see it, it's delegate or die."

I got a sprinkling of applause from the Bronson Alcott contingent. A few of the bus-girls joined in. I flashed them a luminous smile and continued. "Allison, why not let me help you with this?"

She set her clipboard down on the bunk railing and put her fists on her waist. I was so glad she knew where to find it. "You think you can organize this activity?" she challenged.

"Can a leopard change its spots?" De challenged back.

Allison gave her a look. "Not really," she said.

"Well, yes, I *can* organize this activity," I interrupted them. "And, if you like, I can do your colors, too. Khaki is not as neutral as you'd think, believe me. Okay, now, people," I called again, "who here shops primarily Eddie Bauer, the Gap, the Nature Company, and GNC? Okay, Alana, Baez, you, you, you, and—you . . ." I'd seen her get off the bus. She'd had like a hatchet strapped to her backpack. "And you are?"

"Jody," she said.

"Okay, Jody, you're in charge of the campfire girls. Whoever didn't get majorly grossed by *Moby Dick* or really likes sushi or Brad Pitt in *A River Runs Through It*, come with us."

Chapter 4

The lake was sparkling in the sunlight. The water was so clear, you could practically read the labels on the soda pop cans nestled in the mud. Schools of teeny fish skittered between the crumpled cans, disintegrating paper products, and biodegradable fruit rinds beneath the surface.

"I'm glad you decided to stay," Ian said. He was wearing a basic denim shirt. But all bleached out and authentically frayed with the sleeves rolled up to show his excellent cuts, it looked chronic—and way ecological. "The program's really good. I was afraid you'd give up on us too soon."

"Giving up is so not me," I explained. "I've already had some extremely inspirational ideas about redoing our cabin. I'd love to discuss them with you when we have a moment. I fully respect professional input."

"It'll be my pleasure," Ian promised.

"Excuse me," De said. "Is that something edible sticking out of your shirt pocket?"

"You hungry?" He offered her the granola bar, which she immediately devoured. Then, when everyone was gathered around him, Ian popped the lid on the bait can.

De went viciously ashen. In fact, glimpsing the gnarled and writhing worm world at the bottom of the pail, many of us had a similar reaction. A hurl-fest seemed inevitable. "And that is?" Dionne demanded, squinching her eyes shut and pointing at the container.

"That's just bait." Grinning with goodwill, Ian handed us each a no-frills fishing rod. "I'm going to show you how to bait your hooks in a sec. It's much easier—"

"I don't think so," our friend Ariel cut him off. "Unless those things are going to impale themselves on my pole of their own free will."

"If a fish eats a worm, then I'm supposed to eat that fish? As if !" I said. "Don't you have like bread crumbs or something?"

In addition to being a monster hunk, Ian turned out to be furiously sensitive and supportive. He volunteered to bait all our hooks. While he did Ariel's worm, De and I waited for him at the marshy edge of the lake.

"All that trash in the water, that is so bogus," De said feelingly.

"Yeah, I know," I agreed. "I was just standing here thinking, wouldn't it be so dope if there were like housekeeper fish? And, you know, like they'd come in twice a week and clear out all this tragic stuff."

My need for order overcame me. Instinctively, I

reached down and plucked a slimy Coca-Cola can out of the frigid water. Then De scooped up a mushy paper cup. The next thing we knew, Ariel was holding a dripping, old potato chip bag by two fingertips, going: "Ian, Ian. Is there like a trash receptacle around here?" Eyeing the bait can, she added, "Preferably one that does not contain moving parts."

Fishing turned out to be so fun. At least that's what the girls who did it said, while I and my toxic-waste-cleanup crew tidied the shallow waters. The lake must've been fed by a monster glacier. Our hands were blue with cold and in vital need of a breakthrough in skin care technology.

Ian and the fishergirls were way successful. Numerous denizens of the deep were caught. With nothing but scales to warm them, their mass exodus from the frigid depths was not all that surprising. I thought it would be furiously fun, as well as environmentally sound, if like the Pet Factory in Westwood decided to offer trout thermals or little faux fur surfer suits for carp and perch.

After we dragged the green plastic bag Ian had supplied to this big Dumpster in the woods, we all looked through his nature book and tried to identify the fish by brand name.

"Look, it says that one's a speckled trout." De was way impressed with the catch. "Did you ever order that at Spago or Chaya Brasserie?" she asked. "Do you even know how expensive it is!"

Cleaning the fish could have led to another brutal crisis, but Ian's flexible management style averted it. He called for volunteers. Cassandra Gonzales and Marti

Webber from West Covina jumped in. Both of them had previous fish-prep experience. By the time they'd filleted the third trout, the rest of us had gotten past the urge to spew and were willing to wield a gutting knife.

I have to say the campfire girls were way impressed when my posse marched up the hill with the catch of the day.

And I was so proud of Ian. "Is there anything he can't do?" I asked this girl Sydney, who'd come from Santa Monica.

She had an awesome face and figure, with long shaggy-cut platinum curls trailing down her back. "Well, he can't tell when someone's flirting with him," she said. "I've been trying to snag his attention since we got here. And, as you see," she said, indicating her attributes with a seductive spin, "I'm so not easy to ignore."

It was true. Sydney was way reminiscent of Pamela Lee on *Baywatch,* and she had the bad-babe look of Corey Teller's girlfriend on De's fave teen soap, *Coronado Cove.*

I filed this insight on Ian, then De and I snagged excellent seats for the luau. Oscar's foraging crew had delivered heaps of luncheon greens. They were all, "And this one's dandelion, which we found beside the otter dam near the chipmunk grazing field, and the curly-leafed plant is like kale."

But we just dug in. We were so hungry we couldn't have cared less how many tick-and-lice-ridden hooves had tramped across our mesclun leaves. The presentation wasn't much—paper plates, paper napkins—but everything tasted way decent. Especially the pan-seared fish. "This is just like the Ivy," De said, referring to one of Hollywood's foremost celebrity power-snack palaces. "Only without attitude."

Ian came by. I patted the log we were sitting on, and he graciously flopped down between us.

"What a jammin' *dejeuner*," De said, squishing over to make room for him. "You're in college, so you must know what that means, right?"

Ian shrugged his hunky shoulders. "Sounds French."

"Totally!" De shrieked. "You are so def. It *is* French. It means 'lunch.' You're the best." She started pounding Ian's arm enthusiastically. "Is he the best, Cher? Is he fully props?"

I nibbled a wild raspberry and observed her silently for a moment. Dionne was on the verge of full-blown infatuation. I recognized the warning signs: high-pitched adulation combined with coquettish physical contact.

"Almost as vibrant as Murray," I reminded her.

Ian laughed again. "You were both a terrific help today. You really surprised me."

De beamed. "You thought we were just these beautiful, spoiled rich kids. And that we'd like just expect everything handed to us on a silver platter. Like how often have we heard that, right, Cher? As if we were that shallow."

"Not even!" I protested. "So, Ian, this is what I was thinking vis-à-vis the cabin. First of all, De and I could use some real closet space. I mean, if we're going to do any entertaining, that rope thing'll be a major embarrassment." I brushed off my hands and tossed my disposable dinnerware into the trash bag Summer was circulating.

"Hiiii, Ian," she crooned as she went by.

"Hey, Summer," Ian said. "The salad was great."

De rolled her eyes. "She is so obvious," she whispered to me.

"Also, Ian, we're stuck way out in the woods," I continued. "So that unhinged screen door is like an embossed invitation for local wildlife to party on the premises. Plus I've already ruined my best strappy heels on the porch. I don't even want to know what's under there."

"Would you like me to stop by later and have a look at it?"

"Oh, Ian, that'd be the bomb!" De enthused. "Say four-ish?"

"I've got some chores to do. Would after dinner be okay?"

"Excellent," I said.

Ian got up. "Thanks again for helping get things rolling today."

De's smile faded the minute he was gone. "I was way too needy, right?" she asked, nibbling on her bottom lip.

"You know what's whack?" I said. "I don't think he even realizes how choice he is. He's like a total contradiction in terms—a Baldwin without narcissism. Speed-dial the Smithsonian, girlfriend. What a find."

"I can't believe Campanile doesn't deliver," De was complaining. "I mean, my mother eats there three times a week. You'd think they'd have recognized our name." She dropped her cell phone onto her bed and crossed the tragically expensive West Hollywood restaurant off her list.

Expecting Ian any minute, we were still rampantly short on hors d'oeuvres. And dinner had seriously reeked. We were spared the campfire but had to make our own peanut butter and jelly sandwiches. Like from scratch!

Okay, they were fresh—that's fresh as in brand-new, not fresh as in excellent. And De and I had lucked out. We were on the spreading team. But the foraging crew had been forced to shell buckets of peanuts and then had to grind them down to the aforementioned butter. Another group picked, boiled, and squished berries for the jam. I have to say, I have new respect for the Smucker's people. Anyway, we utterly gobbled every calorie-laden morsel. And now, in addition to having a guest to feed, we were hungry again.

Summer answered our all-points bulletin. She stopped by with some party mix her stepmother had tossed into her backpack. "The Palm does a fun feed. Did you try them yet?" she suggested. She was on the floor, lounging on one of my mattresses, which we'd cleverly converted to a futon by propping it against the wall.

"The Palm is majorly carnivore. It's like a contradiction in terms to do steak at a spa," I protested.

"How about Ed Debevic's," Baez offered. "Their meatloaf's chronic."

"Listen, why don't you, Summer, and the rest of the crew come back later tonight? We'll do a slumber fete after Ian makes this place presentable," I said, leading them to our broken screen door.

"Phat," said Summer. The four of us stood on the

porch for a couple of minutes, watching the sunset. It was totally Disney. We hung there, bathed in this blinding Magic Kingdom glow. Then Baez said, "Okay, we're Audi. See you in the P.M."

"Summer," I called from the porch. "We'll still need snacks. Try the Hard Rock. If they don't take Amex, I've got Visa Gold."

As daylight dwindled, De lit our candles and shook her head in front of the makeup mirror. "So what do you think? Should I tie back my extensions or just go relaxed?"

Her cell phone rang before I could respond. It was Murray. I knew because De's hand flew to her hip, her voice went into attitude overdrive, and her face just beamed.

"Nice of you to beep me every twenty-four hours or so," she began, sliding down onto one of the futons. "Yes, I'm glad you called. No, I am not your woman—and I find your growing vocabulary of urban street slang daunting and demeaning—"

There was a knock at the door, followed by a shrill squeak of rusty hinges. "Anybody home?" Ian called.

I signalled De. She nodded and gave me a little wave, indicating that she'd be on the line awhile. "Hey, Ian. Zup?" I said. "Come on in."

He had a toolbox with him and odd bits of lumber, including a long wooden rod that seemed destined to become a closet bar. I was so moved.

Dionne was on the phone with Murray for the entire time that Ian and I discussed domestic improvements. "Do you think we could get a couple of extra blankets and sheets here—you know, just something to drape the mattresses in? I think our best bet is a spare

Japanese effect. Futons, tatami mats, fragrant woods, candles."

He agreed. We nibbled a little of Summer's party mix, swigged Evian and Perrier, and then went to work.

In record time our porch door no longer squeaked or swung weirdly from its hinges. In addition to the wooden rod to replace the closet rope, Ian also put up a nice toiletry shelf. He'd brought cedar chips to scent the cubbies and suggested we gather fragrant sprigs of juniper and eucalyptus for aesthetic as well as aromatic purposes. I just want to say that was a brilliant suggestion. The area around our cabin was rampant with fragrant fallen branches.

Then, as he was about to leave, Ian spotted a wasps' nest on the corner of our porch.

"Murray!" De shrieked into the phone. "There are wasps here! No, not *that* kind of wasp." She looked at me and rolled her eyes. "He thinks I was talking about like White Anglo-Saxon Protestants. Doy, we're out here in the woods. I'm talking about wildlife, Murray, not voting blocs."

"So after all our work, I guess we'll have to move, right?" I asked Ian. "I'm fully heartbroken. Except for the outdoor plumbing—which is so Jurassic—I feel we truly transformed a piece of low-end real estate into a trippin' little bungalow."

Ian laughed. "Stay where you are. I'll just move the nest."

"Not even!" I blurted in disbelief.

"I've got gloves. I'll do it very carefully," he assured me. The flaming twilight was turning a deep, star-studded purple. It was getting dark fast. But Ian hopped up onto our shaky porch railing and gingerly removed the little mud hut. Wasps circled the nest in his hands, but true to his word, Ian was methodical and cautious.

De said a long, affectionate good-bye to Murray and joined me. We watched Ian's progress from the safety of our renovated screen door.

As he disappeared into the woods, she said, "Is he not golden?"

"A brutal hottie," I concurred.

We were both about to breathe a sigh of relief when we heard Ian howl.

We grabbed each other and jumped up and down going, "What are we going to do? What are we going to do? We could be next."

Ian came back sucking on his finger. "They got me," he said, trying to make light of it, but he was dewy-eyed with pain. "The stinger's still in there. My hand's going to blow up unless I get it out. Have you got tweezers or anything?"

"Anything? We've got everything!" I said.

De was already rummaging through her cosmetic case.

By candle and flashlight, we plundered Ian's finger. De was nipping at the swollen red knuckle with her tweezers. "I can't get it," she said finally, bitterly frustrated.

"I have the best idea," I said. "We can rip it out with wax strips! Then cleanse it with Ralph Lauren Coolessence Body Spray!"

It was a brilliant plan. Ian was abjectly grateful. "Do

you know the fable about the lion and the mouse?" he asked, after I had saturated his knuckle with Lauren. We were sitting on the steps of the cabin.

"Lion and the mouse?" I looked at De. We were all: Did they do it in Claymation? Was it Disney? Sound track by Elton John?

"It's a story about a lion," Ian said, pausing to blow on his hand. "Boy, that feels a lot better. Okay, so this lion thought he was king of the jungle. But he was captured by hunters. They tied him up and he was completely helpless. Until a little mouse came along and gnawed through the ropes to set him free."

I thought I understood where he was heading with this. "Like you knowing everything there is to know about nature and wasp nests, right? So that would make you king of the jungle . . . until one of them stings you."

"Oh, I get it," De said, not sure if she liked the comparison. "And we're what—like rodents on a rescue mission?"

"That was just a long and, I guess, not very amusing way of saying I'm in your debt," Ian said, with a way decent smile. "You know, I really came here tonight to thank you for your help today. Cleaning out the lakefront was such a beautiful gesture, and the way you helped organize the girls and got everyone involved . . . I felt this was the least I could do."

"Oh, it was!" De gushed. "The very least. Cher has excellent leadership qualities. And if I hadn't been faint with low blood sugar today, I'd certainly have made a difference, too."

"We're dedicated to that," I explained. "In fact, our young lives are littered with grateful classmates whose ordinary days we've altered and brightened—and you'd be surprised how resistant some people can be."

"We've both been acknowledged for our many special gifts and contributions—primarily in the areas of make-overs and romantic pairings. In all honesty," De said thoughtfully, "I'd have to say, at our school, in terms of popularity, we're basically unchallenged."

"Speaking of which," I ventured, "if you should ever need our services, we are seriously decent match-makers."

"I believe it." Ian gave us one of his ruggedly dazzling smiles.

"So, have you like landed the Betty of your dreams?" De probed.

"She means do you have, you know, a girlfriend," I elaborated.

Ian blushed. And it was not merely the glow of the lantern he was holding reflected on his classic face. "What I really wanted to say is, I still owe you. Listen, you guys better get some rest."

"I take it you're taken?" De pressed.

"Not really," he said. "Hey, no kidding, you're going to be getting up pretty early tomorrow. There are some full days ahead."

"Highlights are?" I asked, walking Ian to the steps.

"Hiking, rafting, rappelling—"

"Repelling? That sounds interesting. What do we repel?"

He thought I was kidding. "Get some rest," he repeated. "Oh, and I left you a flashlight in case you need to use the latrine at night. If you hear animal noises out there, just beam the light around or bang the latrine door loudly. That ought to do it."

My mouth fell. "That ought to do what?" I asked Dionne as Ian disappeared into the darkness with a rubber-soled crackling of twigs and leaves. "What kind of animals do you think he was talking about?"

"Nothing big or long or furry or scaly or clawed, I hope. Maybe that's what we're going to learn to repel tomorrow."

Chapter 5

*U*nless you've lived it, you have no idea how scarring it is to be awakened by the shrill screech of a whistle in the middle of the night. I sat up gasping.

"Who? What?" De murmured.

"What time is it?" I reached out into the dark.

"Don't get up, Cher," Ariel urged me, panicked. "I'm sleeping on the floor right next to your bed."

"Eeeewww! I stepped on a Chicken McNugget!" This from Summer. "I hope!"

Baez moaned. Then she shrieked, "Aaaiiiee! There's someone in here! Look at the door! Look at the door!"

A thin gray light had begun to filter into the room, revealing an indistinct yet threatening silhouette in the doorway. It was big and hunched angrily. We all started screaming at once.

"What are you all doing in here?" the voice from the

doorway demanded. "Why aren't you in your own cabins?"

It was Allison.

There was a mad scrambling. Baez and Ariel were trying to find their shoes. "We were just, you know, visiting. We're on our way back, honest."

"Excuse me," I said. "Do you know that it is considered emotionally abusive and psychologically damaging to wake children in the middle of the night?"

"We learned that in our health class, too," Alana said excitedly. "Unless it's like a major emergency like an earthquake or fire or flood or some other costly natural disaster for which you can't even get homeowner's insurance unless you're a gazillionaire."

"Alana's father is a TV newscaster so she should know," De affirmed.

"It's morning," Allison said. "Five A.M."

"Five A.M.! In what world?" I demanded.

There was some discussion about whether five A.M. could legitimately be called morning or whether community standards should be applied.

"Get dressed, get washed up, and get down to my cabin!" Allison ended the debate.

"But, Allison," De said, "where are we supposed to get washed up? There's no water up here."

"Bull's-eye, Dionne," Allison responded callously. "If there's no water where you are, then you have to go to where the water is," she said, and stalked away.

"What was that, like a Zen koan?" Baez, whose mother does yoga at the Open Center, asked. "You know, like some kind of spiritual riddle?"

We should have taken Ian's advice. Instead, we'd thrown a late-night bender catered by McDonald's, which turned out to be the only place that would agree to deliver to a parking lot.

While woofing Big Macs like heifers—to the sounds of Smashing Pumpkins on Ariel's CD player—we'd done about a half hour on Allison. Consensus was she needed to shed twenty, get a good henna rinse, burn her wardrobe, and engage a full-time personal shopper.

The crew had turned out to be Oscar-friendly. Even those who'd survived the Crushing of the Berries agreed that he was your basic underpaid, overworked, amiable educator, a kind of outdoorsy Mr. Hall.

Ian had scored highest in all categories: from time spent discussing to most desirable attributes. My own observations had strengthened what Sydney, the babe from Santa Monica, had said earlier in the day: Ian seemed heedless of his own hunkdom and surprisingly unaware of the drooling reflex he activated in others.

"This is so not a spa," Summer said now, slipping into her baby blue stack-heel loafers.

"I figured that out after we mashed all that peanut butter," Ariel said wistfully. She'd drawn foraging duty. "I asked Allison what their massage service extension was and she gave me this look."

"Oh, no!" De screamed. We all spun to face her.

"What? WHAT!" everyone started yelling.

"I just figured out what she meant. The *lake!* She wants us to wash up in *the lake!*"

"As if!" I said.

"Not even!" said Baez.

Then we looked at one another and realized that De was right. So then we all started screaming at once.

Washing up was grievous and probably flouted some child welfare statute or other. The lake was way icier than any of us remembered. Allison explained that this was because the sun hadn't warmed it yet.

"And you knew this?" I demanded.

It wasn't just the fact that every artery in my body was contracting with cold and cutting off a vital blood supply to my brain, but extreme temperatures are viciously damaging to your complexion.

"If you were stranded in the wilderness," she said, "you wouldn't have many other options."

"Oh, right, that would be my first thought," Baez grumbled. "Like I'd really die of shame if some raccoon or coyote caught me with dirty hair."

"Speaking of hair," said De, who was so full of goose bumps she was practically Braille. "My conditioner is totally clumping with cold."

At least we didn't have to catch breakfast in our bathwater. Oscar boiled up some oatmeal, which was viciously filling, and Allison seemed to have a way with pan-fried biscuits, and of course there was plenty of homemade jam left. We defrosted around a cozy campfire and then got the good news that Ian was going to lead the morning's hike.

So everyone was all, what am I going to wear, and should I break out my Timberlands or Hush Puppies, and do you think steel-toe Dr. Martens are too urban?

De and I browsed our rack and cubbies. Dionne got into an Austrian mountain-climbing thing with cute suede suspender shorts and an excellent mint wool vest from Chanel Boutique—plus knee socks and these classic all-weather boots she'd picked up in Vail. I opted for a silk mock-turtleneck and side-zip pants from Banana Republic. And then of course I'd bought these hot new lace-up boots at Re-Mix on Melrose, only they were a tiny bit loose because they didn't come in half sizes. They'd felt okay in the store. Which was of course free of gravel, dirt, and twigs—unlike the craggy venue we were scheduled to tackle.

By sunup, we were crashing through the underbrush of whatever the California equivalent of Mount Everest is. You expected snow, nosebleeds, or the grisly remains of an air disaster around every bend. I was in brutal need of a break. "How random is this?" I said to De. "The only locale in the nation without a Starbucks, and we have to climb it."

"I'd kill for a snack," she agreed.

"Don't even say that." Summer shuddered.

"That's probably this afternoon," Alana suggested. "Like first comes harvesting the grapes. Then comes killing for snacks."

We'd been trekking for under an hour when what had been minor shoe discomfort became excruciating pain. I fell behind the others and unlaced my boots and tore off my knee-highs. My pedicure was disaster, and I had blisters the size of the biosphere on both my heels.

Ian was fabulous as usual. Instead of buggin' over my footwear naïveté, he used the opportunity to show us how to make a Native American-type stretcher out of branches and blankets. Only no one had a blanket, so he—literally—gave me the shirt off his back. It was one of his supreme flannels, a blue-and-green tartan thing that looked choice with my eyes. And he had a T-shirt underneath, so while it disappointed those who were eager to scope Ian's pecs, basically it didn't fall into any gray areas of decency. So Ian tied his sturdy XL-size shirt to the poles, and then Baez and Ariel kind of schlepped me around for a while.

We broke early due to my injury. Also Baez accidentally stepped on a spider and went into a total rant about bad karma. And Jody of the hatchet got viciously lashed by some thorny shrub that Alana had rashly let snap. Alana took total responsibility. Not only did she apologize, she pulled a vial of L'Oreal facial astringent out of her Fendi bag and like purified the wound.

I was devastated to learn that I'd have to sit out the morning's whitewater rafting event, especially when everyone came back soaked and shivering. But after a peek at my bruises, Allison whipped out the polysporin ointment and assured me that I'd be riding the rapids by late afternoon—which was when the next victim brigade was scheduled to depart.

I actually had a nice little chat with Allie. We were sitting on the steps of her cabin. Oscar was reading nearby, as usual, I noticed.

"You know you have monster eyes, totally tubular," I told her. "A set of contacts and the lightest touch of enriching lash-lengthener would truly bring them alive. Do you ever wear foundation? Because for someone who's outdoors a lot you've got basically excellent skin, and a decent finishing powder could make the light work to your advantage."

"I don't usually wear makeup," she asserted. "I'm into ecology and my mother is an animal rights activist. And cosmetics companies use a lot of animal products—"

"That totally reeks," I said. "I knew that, though. I read a lot. The Body Shop has excellent educational material on these things. I and my friends are extremely committed to PC makeup whenever it's on sale. So if you do decide to go with a light base, I was thinking, Estee's got this blazing oil-control hydrator that totally prevents makeup from migrating."

She was surprisingly open to suggestions. I started to put two and two together and realized that Oscar Epstein's proximity was not coincidental. Oscar and Allie were, if not already an item, a romantically correct possibility.

"Have you ever had your colors done?" I asked her, glancing significantly at the supine, reading Oscar.

"I don't think so. I'm afraid I've always chosen comfort over style. I'm basically a pragmatic person."

"Style *is* pragmatic," I said, shocked. "I mean, there's nothing you can't get if you look good. It's majorly basic. Let's get your colors done. I'll dial my person in town and have him pull a chart for you. I bet it comes back saying auburn is your number one hair tint choice."

It was an excellent bonding session, but Allison had chores to attend to. So while the polysporin did its work, I was sent lakeside to serve in Ian's sushi-harvesting crew.

I actually caught a fish for lunch. It was this really cute perch. Ian showed us a new wormless technique that involved faking out the future morsels by making lures out of found objects. It was way creative and extremely ecological.

I limped around gathering fallen feathers and colorful leaves with Dionne and a couple of other girls, including Sydney, the *Baywatch* goddess from Santa Monica. Then Ian had us do this little arts and crafts thing. We tied the feathers and leaves together, adding beads and other fish-enticing shiny objects. Ian said that even dangly earrings could be used in a pinch.

I thought, oh right, you bring the hook, I'll bring the Cartier teardrops. Not even!

But Sydney whipped off her hanging rhinestones and handed them to him. "If there's anything else you need—anything at all," she crooned, batting her lash extenders at Ian, "don't hesitate to ask."

In addition to her tumbling platinum locks and other Pamela Lee–type attributes, Sydney's woodland ensembles were a page out of the Victoria's Secret catalog, lingerie division. At the moment, she was dressed for fly-casting success in red satin boxers and a black lace halter top. Sydney was wild for Ian. And, as her wardrobe choices hinted, subtle was so not her strength.

She pulled up her hair and said she thought she'd left her halter snap open in the back and could he do it for her. He said no, it looked closed. A minute later she was back with, "No really, it feels open." What a surprise—it was!

Ian said, "De, Ariel? Could one of you help Sydney?"

She said, "But I want you to do it, Ian."

He said, "Not really. My hands are full of fish."

Then she was all, "Oooo, Ian, there's something in

my eye. Could you look at it, please?" Her prime-time face was raised expectantly.

He told her to hold her lid and blink. And all this time he was like whistling and smiling and checking lures and helping people reel in their catches.

De and I pondered them briefly while we fished.

"Is Ian modest, shy, or truly oblivious?" De asked.

"Maybe just selective," I proposed.

Chapter 6

The high cost of romantic obsession became obvious to us during our afternoon rafting expedition. And further clues to Ian's cluelessness began to surface.

After lunch, Allison distributed our white-water gear—life vests, shiny waterproof ponchos, and rain hats. All suited up, we looked like a convention of frozen-crab-cake fishermen.

"Excuse me," Sydney said as Ariel scrambled into the front of the rusty old BHNE van. "That's my seat you're in. See, Ian will be there—" She pointed to the empty driver's seat beside Ariel. "And I'll be here," she said, "where you used to be."

"I have to sit up front," Ariel protested. "I get

"No problem," Sydney said, "since this is not a car—it's a van."

By the time Ian arrived, the Baywatcher was in the bucket seat of her choice, freshening her garish lip gloss in the rearview mirror.

De was outraged. I was way impressed.

Rarely had I seen such single-minded determination outside aerobics class. The girl must have had a personal trainer in pushiness. "She's desperately needy," I consoled Ariel.

Ian drove us several miles farther up the dusty road our limo had traveled. By the time we arrived at the rafting site, Ariel was ready to blow chunks. Within minutes, most of us were prepared to join her. We climbed out of the van and stared in rabid disbelief at Nature's own Jacuzzi raging before us.

There were a couple of rubber rafts sitting on a pebbly stretch of beach. And then there was the water. The fierce river had little in common with our placid lake. It was stocked with boulders against which the water slapped and churned. The occasional branch sailed past—not your skinny little campfire twig, but like a total arm of a tree—and the way it crashed and banged and twisted and tore its way along the river seemed like a bitter preview of what awaited us.

"Smashing against rocks out here in Desolation State Park is not my idea of a fun afternoon," I told De.

"Excuse me," she said, waving at Ian. "Will someone please tell me what this destructive force of nature has to do with confidence and self-esteem?"

Ian laughed. "It's about mastering the elements," he said.

"You know, learning how to survive in different environments—doesn't that give you self-confidence?" Jody suggested.

"Hitting a rock in a rubber raft is a seriously harsh way to build confidence," I pointed out. "Hitting an end-of-season sale at a boutique in Sunset Plaza is way more satisfying—plus you can get a decent wardrobe out of it."

"Yes," De agreed. "And anyway, some elements are better left unmastered."

Ian was setting oarlocks into the raft. "Come on," he said. "It's not as bad as it looks. And Jody's right, these exercises stretch you: emotionally, physically—some think even spiritually."

"Details on the physical aspect," I requested, the teensiest bit intrigued.

"Steering is pretty strenuous," he began, tossing the oars into the raft and pulling it toward the water. "You'd be strengthening and toning biceps, triceps, lats, and abs. Your stomach muscles really tighten up, and your quadriceps get a great workout—that's the front of the thigh. You know, women tend to store more fat directly under the skin around the thighs than men do, so it's especially important to keep the thigh muscles as strong as possible. Strong leg muscles prevent overlying fat and skin from sagging—"

We were piling into the boat even as he spoke.

After a briefing on navigation and ballast, Ian joined us. "Hold on, we've got to redistribute the weight here," he said as we bobbed in the shallows. "Cher, Jody, and Sydney, you're center. Dionne and Baez, up front. Ariel, you're the littlest. You're back here with me."

"Don't tell me you get raftsick, too," Sydney said as she and Ariel swapped seats again.

We pushed off into the current. Ian was right, of course. It wasn't as scary as it had seemed. We kind of moved and bobbed in ecological harmony with the river. Ian showed Ariel how to work the rudder. Sydney kept glancing over her shoulder at them and forgetting to use her oar. Fortunately, I turned out to be furiously oar-adept and was able to compensate for her sloppy paddling.

We didn't hit the rocks but the water did, hard. It splashed up at us every few feet. The gear Allison had given us kept our bodies pretty dry, but our faces were regularly sprayed with foam.

"This is so not amusing," Sydney sputtered.

One of her lash extenders was hanging loose like a wet spider. "Lancôme makes a fabulous all-weather mascara," I hinted. "It's frantically waterproof."

"How def is this!" Ariel was hollering happily, in fierce contrast to Sydney's discontent. "This is a totally jammin' experience. I feel way spiritual!"

"That does it," Sydney said to me. "I'm going back there."

"Okay, now, things are going to get a little wilder around this bend," Ian shouted.

"Hello, Sydney. You cannot get up now," I pointed out. "You'll fully destroy our balance."

Try talking safety to a woman obsessed. She

brutally ignored me. As Ian predicted, we swerved crazily around a turn in the river, and all of a sudden we were cruising Demolition-land. Giant craggy boulders jutted viciously out of the water, totally dwarfing the everyday terrifying rocks we'd navigated through.

"Your life may be disposable," I shouted above the water's roar, "but I am young, beautiful, and college bound! So sit down this minute, Sydney, before you derail my future and lose your eyelashes."

Rocking wildly and trying to grab one of our oarlocks for balance, Sydney abruptly announced over the water's roar that she was trading seats with Ariel or else.

"Get down!" Ian shouted at her.

"Get up!" Sydney ordered Ariel, who was hanging over the rudder, all green and hyperventilating.

We hit a branch. The front of the raft flew up. Sydney did this windmill thing with her arms. I'd just gotten two juliettes repaired, but there was no time for nail vanity. I snagged her poncho and held on with both hands while she lunged around the raft.

Somehow, Ian steered us through the rock soup. Jody took over my oar; De took over Sydney's. We made it to the shore.

"Do you even know how tragic this could have been!" I shouted at Sydney. "It took two hours to have these nails done! Do you have a hint how expensive Valerie Beverly Hills is?"

After that treacherous episode, I decided it was time to do a chat with Ian. He wasn't dumb about most things, but I felt he'd gone way beyond blond here.

That evening, De and Baez pulled egg-gathering duty down at the hen house. I foraged with Oscar's troop, and after an excellent herb omelet experience, I had my heart-to-heart with Ian.

We were sitting on the steps of the Crypt. De was inside, cordlessly connecting with Murray. I could hear her telling him of the day's adventures. She sounded way proud of what we'd survived.

If there was anything De had always possessed in abundance it was confidence. But there was a certain something in her voice that night that definitely suggested increased self-esteem. The Beverly Hills Nature Experience was working, I marveled. It was forcing growth upon us—and I don't just mean from fat-rich peanut butter and cholesterol-burdened eggs.

"De and I learned a lot today," I confided to Ian. "I want to thank you for the way you've supported us in this our first spa experience."

"No, no, no. It's you I owe thanks to," he said, with Baldwinian modesty. "If you hadn't grabbed that girl today, someone could have gotten seriously hurt."

" 'That girl'? Do you even know her name?"

He scratched his head—he really did. "Um . . . Sydney, right? She's one of the kids from Santa Monica?"

" 'One of the kids'? She's a femme fatale, Ian. A fatal attraction. She has the biggest crush on you."

"No way," he said.

"Do you even know how attractive you are?"

"Me? Come on." He actually blushed.

"Ian, can I be frank with you?" I asked, not waiting for the go-ahead. "You know I'm a fan. I think you're a solid hottie, but your cluelessness almost got us killed today. Can't you tell when someone's brutally flipped for you?"

He shrugged. "Guess not."

"Is it because you're not interested in girls?"

"No, that's not it," he said. "In fact, I *am* interested in a girl. There's this girl who doesn't know I'm alive—"

"Right, like you'd be a good judge of that," I said sarcastically.

"I'm interning on one of her dad's projects in this work-study program at school. But if you want to know what my real problem is, when I meet someone I like, I can't even talk to her—"

"Oh, that's flattering," I said. "Since you have no trouble talking to me."

He laughed. "Cher, you're the easiest person to talk to I've ever met. But when I'm, you know, *interested* in someone, it gets totally weird. I can't speak. I get stupid. I trip all over myself."

"That is so fixable!" I said. "De and I are way expert at romance management and dating strategies. World class." I stifled a yawn. We'd been up for hours, performing bruisingly exhausting events, and I was seriously tired.

He stood up. "You're falling asleep," he noted. "You must be really wiped out. Thanks again for today. You'd better turn in now. Big day tomorrow."

"Not another one," I gasped.

He nodded and did his irresistible laugh. "Toughest yet. Rappelling."

The next day, after a brisk sunrise dip and a final campfire breakfast, we tackled rappelling. Oscar and Allison were our tour guides. We learned from them that rappelling, as opposed to repelling, involved tying a rope around your bod and swinging down the face of a mountain. For De, who gets nosebleeds riding the Century Plaza's outdoor elevators, this did not promise a fun morning.

"Frankly, after all we've been through," I told her, "throwing myself over a cliff seems anticlimactic."

Allison must have heard me.

"Why do I have to go first?" I asked, as she led me to the jumping-off spot at the edge of a dizzying crevice overlooking the Pacific.

"You're a natural leader, Cher. If you do it, the others will follow."

"And if this fragile string you're fastening around my waist snaps and I plummet a thousand feet into that cactus-filled canyon below, they won't, right? Not a persuasive argument, Allie. Although I do want to say that your eyes look seriously transformed."

"Oscar said so, too," she confided, testing the play of the rope through the pulley on my harness. "It's the lash lengthener you loaned me. Do you think it's working?"

Dionne and the other lemmings were waiting with Oscar near the van. He was tying on Sydney's rig. She was next up, and from the way she'd acted at breakfast—like she'd dropped my oatmeal, then scooped it out of the dirt and plopped it back in my bowl—I gathered she was miffed at me. Sydney had decided I was Ian's favorite, and she was way cranky over it.

I turned my attention back to Allison. "Also, that translucent face powder's chronic," I told her. "When's your appointment for lenses?"

"Week from Tuesday. Oscar's going to drive me there. Then afterward, I'm hitting the Beverly Center. The personal shopper you recommended is meeting us at four. Okay, now—" She tugged on the rope. "Are you ready?"

"Would 'No' be a crushing disappointment?"

"You're going to be fine," she promised. "Have you got your speech set for graduation?"

"Yes. Will you read it for me if something whack happens here? Also, you can have the total contents of my entire cosmetic case. Except for the Chanel lip creme, which is way too pale for you. Give that to Dionne. And tell her not to use a dark liner with it. It's a tacky look."

"Nothing's going to go wrong. Ian's halfway down there, see him?"

"What, that tiny speck clinging to the rock wall? I thought it was a chipmunk with a thing for plaid."

She tugged at my line, checked the tension of the rope around the tree trunk, then turned me around and said, "You know what to do."

And I did. I saw De, gave her an encouraging little thumbs-up sign, and stepped backward over the cliff. The rope went whirring through my harness. And I was banging—feetfirst, as instructed—into the frightening rust-colored face of the mountain, descending a couple of yards each time I pushed off. Ian was down below, and he really did seem frantically petite. It was easier to look up. Which was when I saw Sydney above me, getting ready to rappel.

I have to say I put on speed after that. I did not want to be stuck between the *Baywatch* beauty and the object of her obsessive affection. She seemed determined to catch up with me, however. The next thing I knew, she was descending at a hair-raising pace. Literally, her white blond hair was flying every which way. Her hands clutched frantically at the rope. My first instinct was to scramble out of her way. Then I realized that she was out of control.

I glanced down. Ian was shouting something that I couldn't hear. From the top of the cliff, Oscar was gesturing wildly. There was only one thing to do. I whipped out my cellular and dialed De.

"Sydney's descent seems majorly reckless. Ask Allie what the drill is. I'm in need of options, strategies, advice. I could also use a shiatsu massage. I'm like retaining major tension in my shoulders."

De put me on hold for a sec. I pressed speaker-phone, tucked my mobile into my belt, and swung myself in Sydney's direction. "Girlfriend." De was back on the line, speed-speaking breathlessly. "Survey says, 'Reach out and touch someone'!"

Sydney came frantically barreling and bumping along. I caught her, wrapped both arms around her waist, and held on for dear life while, above us, De pumped Oscar for instructions.

"Not you again," Sydney said, with a stranglehold on my neck.

"Gratitude is so not your strength," I remarked. "As

long as we're hangin' here—I've been wanting to chat with you anyway," I said. "This jealousy thing you've got going is way unattractive. First of all, Ian and I are brutally platonic. Just friends. But it would be shabby of me not to confide that there's another Betty in his picture. He's taken, Sydney. There's a babe he's gone on."

"That hurts," she said.

"Look at it as a growth opportunity," I urged. "It's not considered choice to pass your pain along to innocent bystanders. I think your treatment of Ariel yesterday was grim. And forget that oatmeal stunt you pulled this A.M. Brat attacks like that don't exactly send your stock soaring."

I heard Oscar's voice on speakerphone. It was the classic story. Sydney had panicked, but basically she'd been safe all along. I was supposed to buddy with her until the other girls passed us, then talk her down peacefully. If all else failed, Allie would join us and take over from me.

"Oscar says you're fine," I said after I'd clicked off the phone. "In fact, he says you'd have been okay even if I hadn't snagged you."

We were swaying above a thousand-foot gully. "Well, it's the thought that counts," said Sydney. "So thanks for saving my life anyway. Even if you didn't."

"What about yesterday?" I reminded her.

"My false eyelashes!" She started to laugh. "I lost one; the other stuck to my cheek. When I looked in the mirror I thought it was an insect and demolished it. They cost a fortune. I'm like in mourning."

We started to laugh. Which made our ropes jiggle.

So we started to scream. And then we were laughing and screaming and swinging together. When we finally caught our breath, Sydney said, "So what do you think I should do? Apologize to Ariel . . . and then?"

We hung and swung and talked solutions: therapy, support groups, wardrobe and makeup choices—"I'd move away from the lingerie-for-daytime look," I suggested—audio tapes, self-help books . . .

The time flew by. So did our friends, one by one.

Finally Oscar buzzed me again and gave us the all clear. "We're Audi," I told Sydney. And we descended, shrieking and laughing and hugging each other, to thunderous cheers and applause.

That afternoon, before graduation, Ian and I exchanged digits. He said he had a carpentry job coming up, but he'd be beepable in the L.A. area anytime De or I needed an ear. De was over her crush on him, but she was furiously moved when he buzzed her cheek and wished her well. He planted a brotherly kiss on me, too. "Remember, Miss Mouse," he said. "I owe you."

Graduation was poignant.

I in my hot red Alaïa and De in a rayon jersey sheath by Kamali sat on the steps of Allison's cabin, listening to Sydney's speech. We were each supposed to talk about what we'd learned at BHNE. For Sydney, it was the importance of trust, friendship, and waterproof makeup. She said she was enrolling in a Women Who Love Too Much seminar the minute she got home—and wondered if Ian could give her a lift to the first session.

Ariel talked about rappelling. She said it was a real

breakthrough for her. She'd had car sickness all her life, but jumping off the mountain was the first time she'd ever experienced vertical nausea. Then she apologized to Summer, who'd been below her when she spewed.

Summer said she was proud to have learned the difference between porridge and forage. She'd become a total fan of foraging. From now on she was going to insist on fresh fruits and vegetables, and she had new respect for places like Ralph's, and even Von's supermarkets, because they made this excellent food available without your having to lose an acrylic every time you were hungry.

Baez agreed with Summer. She was over being a junk foodie and was seriously thinking about giving up spicy fries.

De had a lot of valuable insights. She ended by saying that she felt physically, mentally, and spiritually stretched, and that the experience had become a lot more to her than just a legal way to blow off phys ed for two weeks. Then she circulated a petition requesting that Ms. Stoeger give us at least a full month off.

"And now," Allison said, when everyone but me had been called on, "at every session we find there are one or two people whose personal growth and contributions to others epitomize what the Beverly Hills Nature Experience is all about. For the leadership qualities she's exhibited, for her unflagging devotion to change—mine as well as everyone else's—for her willingness to accept challenges and overcome obstacles, I'm happy to introduce the girl you all voted

BHNE's highest honor—our Leadership Award winner, Cher Horowitz."

I was overwhelmed. Everyone stood up and clapped. Summer and Baez grew misty-eyed. Sydney did, too, but I think it was because of the way Ian was beaming at me. Even Oscar set down his book and applauded—then he took the radiant Allison's hand. And Dionne, who'd known about this golden event, suddenly produced this classic armful of exceptional wildflowers.

She hugged me and handed me the bouquet.

"How majorly supportive," I said, accepting the gift. "Did you pick them yourself?"

"No, Alana did. That's why she's not here," De explained. "She had an allergy attack and then broke out in some random rash, so she asked me to give them to you."

"They're way choice," I said.

"They're also itchy. I wouldn't hang on to them for too long," she cautioned. "Girlfriend, I am so proud of you."

Then everyone quieted down. You could hear the breeze whooshing through the fir trees. The long grass and dry reeds swayed gently at the lake's edge. The splash of a trout or carp broke the mirrored stillness of the lake, and ripples rolled lazily toward shore.

I cleared my throat and looked at my notes. There were so many festive moments I wanted to recount. But I was too choked with emotion. Plus De was right—the flowers were like Bug World, U.S.A.

"What I've learned here at BHNE," I began, "is that

proper planning, a flexible attitude, a simple yet versatile wardrobe, and a couple of ample suitcases— preferably crafted by the fine Italian leather-workers of Gucci—are the keys to a successful spa experience. You might also consider finding a masseuse who makes rural housecalls and having your parents pre-mail you care packages of goodies. Gift baskets from Mrs. Beasley's in Beverly Hills are hot, but Manhattan Fruitier in West Hollywood also does a dynamite arrangement. There's so much more I could say—I haven't even touched on nails, hair, and skin care. But I see our limo driver waiting and, most of all, I want to go home. So thank you. Thank you all!''

Chapter 7

We returned to the Greater Los Angeles area as twilight and a major smog alert descended on the city. Freeway fumes hung gray and welcoming above the twinkling lights of town. It was majorly dope to be home.

Daddy was so glad to see me. He was all done up in an Armani dinner jacket.

"Daddy, you didn't have to go formal just for me," I said, as Al the limo driver carried in my suitcases.

"It's not for you. I've got an important dinner tonight with a new client—the most important new client of my career." He kissed me on the head and grabbed his scarf. "I'll be out late. We'll talk soon," he said from the door.

Al was halfway up the stairs with my luggage. Daddy's bushy eyebrows met in a fierce frown as he regarded the limo driver. "He's from Exclusivo, right? No tip when you sign the voucher," he said. "They include a fifteen percent service charge. Lock up after him. Good night."

I buzzed Daddy's cheek, locked up after Al, and paused on my way upstairs to say hi to Mom. "I'm home, Ma," I said to the portrait in our domed entrance hall. "Guess what? I was voted a Leadership Award. Cool, huh? Just thought you'd want to know."

Mom died when I was just an infant, but we still have a relationship. She's an excellent listener. Plus her pale eyes in the painting are totally benevolent. They just like pierce through you with compassion.

The message counter on my machine was frantically blinking double digits when I got to my room. The first four messages were from Tai. As I was listening to the playbacks, the phone rang anew. "Cher! You're home! How perfect is that—I call, you're there?"

"*Quel* coincidence. Hi, Tai," I said, flopping with the cordless onto my bed.

"Guess who's hot, popular, and appearing in person at Bronson Alcott High School?" she squealed before I said another word.

"Let me guess? Hot, popular, and making personal appearances? Doy, could it be . . . me," I said.

"No, Corey Teller's sister!"

"Excuse me? Corey Teller, studmuffin star of *Coronado Cove?*"

"Yes!" Tai enthused. "His sister, Mariah, transferred to our school. She started Monday while you guys were up at that spa."

This was radically new, indeed. I sat up abruptly. "Corey Teller?" I repeated. "De is going to viciously bug. Just last month she turned her Wu Tang wall into a virtual Corey Teller shrine. He's her total poster boy. Personally, I like Jake," I said, referring to the *Coronado Cove* bad boy played by the furiously desirable Scott Morrison. "He's got the greatest voice, all scratchy and husky."

"Scott's nimble. But isn't it classic to have Corey's sibling in our class? I mean, Corey's a monster hottie. But Ryder is deeply enamored of his sister. He like worships Mariah."

"Ryder has a thing for the new girl? Condolences," I commiserated, saddened. "Just hang in there, girl-friend. As long as you don't convert your misery into calories, Tai, the pain will pass."

"No, no. It's majorly fine. I'm way impressed with her, too. Wait till you meet her, Cher. She's totally the best! She's like the most beautiful, most popular, most generous—"

"Hello! I'm having a déjà vu flash here," I inter-rupted. "Best? Most? I'm not trying to be all possessive about those superlatives, Tai, but they've frequently been used to describe me. So what exactly do you mean when you say, for example . . . *most* generous?"

"Okay, okay, here's the thing," said Tai. "Mariah's so cool. She's not just rich, Cher, she's a gazillionaire. She's an *important* consumer. A black-belt shopper. She bought me an Anna Sui cotton cardigan—it's like my first real designer sweater!"

"Tai," I objected, "I gave you a fabulous Mizrahi skinny-ribbed T."

"Yeah, but it was yours, and used," Tai said. "This Anna Sui is brand-new and all mine."

I was stung. But my own distress was quickly eased

by a rush of compassion for the new girl. Mariah Teller had obviously felt that she needed to buy Tai's friendship. She sounded way insecure. "Well, if you like the Anna Sui, I'm happy for you, Tai," I said. "Of course, I think Isaac Mizrahi has a lot more to say about style than Anna Sui does. I mean, Anna Sui doesn't even wear a headband."

"You're probably right," Tai said agreeably. "Catch you tomorrow, girlfriend."

"Want a lift to school?"

"Mariah's sending her car for me."

"She's leased a limo to take her to school?" I said.

"It's not leased. She owns it. Her dad doesn't like her to drive. I mean, Mariah has her license and all. And he bought her two monster sports cars. But he'd rather she use the limo. It's a tax thing, I think. See you tomorrow, Cher. I'm glad you're back!"

I had barely begun unpacking when the phone rang again. This time it was Janet Hong. She was majorly excited about my homecoming. I started to describe the BHNE graduation ceremony and how moving it was to have my leadership skills acknowledged. But the usually demure math whiz cut me off.

"Cher, Cher, wait—listen to this. I helped someone at school with a trig problem yesterday, and when I got home today this gorgeous hand-tooled silver box overflowing with fresh-cut flowers, caviar, and chocolate truffles was waiting for me."

"Chronic," I said. "Was there a note?"

"Yes, a thank-you note—in calligraphy! It was from the girl I helped with math. She's new. You haven't met her yet—"

"Initials M.T.?" I asked.

"How did you guess? She's Corey Teller's sister! Her name's Mariah. Don't you think she's frantically thoughtful?"

What I really thought was that a silver box for a trig solution was seriously extreme. I mean, I was happy for Janet. But Mariah Teller's acts of extravagance seemed like transparent, gratitude-groveling ploys to me. I was eager to meet her. She might be, as Tai had suggested, overburdened by popularity and good looks, but I sensed she was crying out for help.

I awoke the next morning in severe hot-roller withdrawal. I had gone for three days without the use of a single contemporary appliance, and now my squeaky-clean, protein-conditioned hair craved curls.

Finding Lucy and helping her whip up a tasty yet nutritious breakfast that Daddy would totally ignore; making sure Rico was on hedge-pruning patrol lest our greenery grow unruly; getting Jose, our Mr. Fix-it, to environmentally sort the garbage and prepare it for pickup; these and dozens of other tasks marked the beginning of my day.

There was so much to do that I left the rollers in too long and had to rearrange my coif at the last moment. I piled my crazily corkscrewed curls up on my head, bound them with a festive ribbon, and took off for school in a towering 'do.

"Phat dreads," Dionne commented when I ran into her in the parking lot. "What made you go ethnic?"

"Is it too brash?" I asked.

"Way tall is all. Wait until you catch my man,

girlfriend." De changed the subject with a huge, prideful smile. "Cher, I am totally kvelling. Something major is brewing at Bronson Alcott, have you heard?"

Just then a fashion statement in flowing white linen trousers and a creamy striped T, with a navy blazer dangling loosely over his shoulders, beeped the alarm on Murray's car. The Baldwin turned to face us, flashing a fabulous gold-free smile.

"Murray?" I gasped.

"Good morning, Cher," said this *GQ* vision with Murray's voice.

"That garb is outstandingly Emporio Armani," I complimented him.

"Thanks," Murray said. "Actually, it's Perry Ellis meets Joop. I'm totally over my Hilfiger thing. I blew out a Gold card at A/X yesterday, and then did some major signing at Neiman's. My new look is basically deconstructed. Shall we?" he asked, extending his arms to De and me.

"Go ahead without us, Murray," De said. "I'm brutally in need of girl talk with my homie. Catch you later."

Murray raised an eyebrow at her. " 'Homie'?" he said, and shook his head. Then he fluffed the silk handkerchief in his breast pocket, gave us a little wave, and sauntered off.

"Girlfriend, to what do we attribute Murray's radical conversion?" I asked, stunned.

"That's what I was just going to tell you." De put her arm through mine and we strolled toward the Quad. "While we were gone, Corey Teller's sister transferred to our school!" she said.

"Mariah."

"Oh, you already know." De's disappointment was fleeting. "Well, you know Corey is the star of *Coronado Cove*—"

"Hello, his picture is only on the cover of *Interview, People, Details,* and every other magazine. Although, I have to say, I find Scott Morrison way more appealing."

Two of my most avid fans, Sean and Christel, passed us at that moment.

"Hello, I'm back," I called, brutally bewildered that they hadn't paused to acknowledge me.

"Hey, Cher, zup?" Sean greeted me over his shoulder.

"Cher, hi!" Christel eyed my hair. "Proper locks," she said. "Gotta run."

"Yeah," said Sean, "we're Audi. Mariah's giving away these choice *Coronado Cove* posters and they're going fast. You know how she is."

"Actually, I don't. De and I have been away—" I began.

"No kidding," said Christel. "I didn't even notice. Catch you later."

De was oblivious to the rebuff. "Corey Teller," she continued when we were alone again, "is the flavor of the month, the year, the decade! He's Keanu, Brad, and Tyson all rolled into one."

"Corey's excellent," I agreed, "but so is Scott."

"But did you realize, girlfriend, that Corey's dad— and this new girl's—is *the* major producer of prime-time teen soaps ever? Haskell Teller. Have you heard of him?"

There was something vaguely familiar about the name. "In passing," I said. "But what's all this got to do with Murray?"

"Well, apparently, this new girl Mariah—Corey Teller's sister—told Murray that her father is trolling for a young guy to play a character part on *Coronado Cove*. She said Murray was perfect for the role—if he'd just lose the street shtick!"

"And she's going to do something to help him, right?" I hadn't met her yet, but Mariah's need to give of herself was surfacing as a predictable theme.

"Yes! How did you know?" De said excitedly. "She promised to introduce him to her dad. And when Murray gets the part, I get to meet Corey Teller! If it happens before I get my new Amex card, will you lend me the plunging black lace tunic you snagged at Gucci for your birthday?"

"De, Murray hasn't even auditioned yet and you're planning your wardrobe?"

"You think it's premature? I don't know. Just the thought of Corey drives me to extreme ensemble fantasies. I can't wait to meet him."

"Well, I'm equally eager to meet his sister," I said.

We were ambling across the Quad now. It was rampant with morning activity. I made myself fully available to greet those who had missed us during our three-day hiatus from school.

People were heading to class, grabbing a latte at the campus bean bar, tossing Frisbees under the palms, skateboarding down the school steps, writing checks for homework answers, speed-dialing cherished friends, and breaking into discussion groups on grades, dating, and weekend custody arrangements. Although the Quad was at maximum student capacity, hardly anyone seemed to notice us.

I mean, we got a few waves, a few whistles, a few apparel-specific compliments. I was in a red rayon micro and sheer silk overshirt; De was having a Dolce & Gabbana kind of day. But among the ardent members of the Crew, our return was not being frantically celebrated.

"De, is it my imagination or is there a mysterious absence of enthusiasm for our homecoming?"

"Now that you mention it," De said, "no one has actually clamored to our side since we set foot on campus."

It was cryptic. The bell rang. The Quad emptied. De and I looked at each other, shrugged, and went to class.

My opener for the day was algebra with Ms. Hanratty. Janet was sitting tall in the front row. A crowd of classmates was lined up at her desk, waiting for her to check and explain their homework.

Jesse was sorting CDs at his desk when I entered. "Cher, Cher, come here," he called, excited to see me. "Madonna phoned me last night," he said, grinning.

"Right," said Hannah DuBrow, our resident teen feminist and New Age guru. "And Roseanne realigned my spine. As if!"

"Cher, hi. Wow, I've missed you!" It was Summer.

I joined her at her desk. Alana was sitting next to her. Her face was bitterly broken out from the wild-flower attack.

"Yesterday seems so long ago, doesn't it?" I said, feeling suddenly nostalgic about the BHNE experience. "I mean, it's as though our lives have changed in some crucial yet nameless way that no one seems to care about but us. Reentry is way more difficult than I imagined," I confided.

"I know. It's like you missed everything, right?" said Alana.

"Not even!" I said. "I feel that I learned so much, that I grew in so many areas—"

"You'll get over it," Summer said. "Did you hear about Corey Teller?"

"What happened to him?" I asked.

"His sister is at our school!" Alana replied.

"Like she's in our class!" Summer added.

"Like in *this* class," Alana said.

"Really? Where is she?" I asked, surveying the roomful of totally familiar faces.

Just then Ms. Hanratty came in, carrying about a thousand books, papers, and other teaching utensils. No one budged. No one hurried to her aid. High school boys are so random. "Sean, Jesse, Mark," I hissed, "where are your manners?"

They turned their heads slowly and stared at me with these bleakly blank expressions. But Hannah and a couple of other girls had leaped to Ms. Hanratty's assistance. And I would have, too, except I knew it would be, like, there goes my juliette.

Mariah arrived fashionably late. And I do mean fashionably.

What happened was, I slid into my regular seat, in front of Jesse, as Ms. Hanratty started taking attendance. She was midway through the roll call when Amber rushed into the room, clutching two backpacks and more books than she'd ever touched before.

"Mariah's here!" she shouted, gasping for breath. "She's coming. Don't mark her tardy."

All eyes turned to the door. Mariah Teller swept in, smiling apologetically.

She was blindingly blond in the Drew Barrymore bad-girl mode. But her brutally bleached, choppy-cut hair had clearly been styled by an exalted name— someone who charged by the follicle. She was also tall, slender, and had decent facial bones—although her narrow nose suggested surgical tampering.

"I am *so* sorry," she gushed. "This is my *absolute* favorite class. My tardiness is *inexcusable*—yet I have to say, it was *furiously* unavoidable. Ms. Hanratty, can you *ever* forgive me?"

I thought it was a two-thumbs-up performance. So did Hanratty. Our stern math teacher was all forgiving smiles. She said, "All right, sit down, dear." This from a woman who normally wouldn't have said *dear* if you'd asked her to describe Bambi's mother.

Anyway, I did an up-close-and-personal on Mariah as she scanned the room for available seating.

The girl was wearing practically an entire issue of *Vogue*. It was mostly Jil Sander—white cotton tank and polyamide "paper-bag" pants, with black-and-white slingback golf shoes by Manolo Blahnik, and a gray Australian-pearl necklace by Angela Pintaldi.

Since I had considered purchasing every item and accessory now accenting Mariah's slender bod, it was easy to do a price-tag tally of her haute couture. I came up with a mid-five-figure tab. Which was way more than De or I would even *think* about spending for school wear. Unless we were dressing for a seriously

special occasion, of course—like a prom or a graduation or a class where the substitute teacher turned out
to be a monster hottie.

All of a sudden, Jesse was stricken with politeness.
He jumped up and offered Mariah his seat. "Madonna
called me last night, just like you promised," he told
her excitedly. "Thanks for giving her my number,
Mariah. Oh, and she said to say hi to your dad."

It traveled around the room like wildfire. You could
hear the whole class going: "Madonna called Jesse.
Mariah gave her his number. She said to say hi to her
father."

Mariah took her backpack and books from Amber,
accepted Jesse's gratitude with a modest smile, and
slid into the seat behind me.

Before I had a chance to introduce myself, I felt an
acrylic tap on my shoulder.

"Excuse me," Mariah whispered politely. "Could
you move just a little. I can't see the board over your
hair."

I was stung and momentarily taken aback. "I had a
hot-roller incident this A.M.," I explained, turning to
face her. "My hair is usually long, silky, and excellent.
We haven't met." I gave her a welcoming smile. "But
I'm sure you've heard of me. I'm Cher."

"Cher?" said Mariah.

"Cher Horowitz," Ms. Hanratty called.

"Here." I raised my hand.

"Oh, *that* Cher," I thought I heard Mariah gasp. I
glanced back over my shoulder at her. Her faux green
eyes widened. They were of an emerald hue not readily
found in nature, so I assumed she was sporting tinted
contacts.

"Are you all right?" Amber rushed down the aisle to her side.

"Of course I am," Mariah said, wincing at her concern and also, I guessed, at the long-haired monkey sweater Amber was wearing. It was this stringy brown bolero that she'd paid a fortune for in a vintage shop on Melrose. Some overweight guy in an antique Hawaiian shirt had foisted it upon her as shabby-chic.

Mariah stared at it now and shook her head. "Didn't we buy the cashmere to replace that thing? Really, I'm fine," she said, waving Amber away.

Then, with new interest, she furiously scrutinized me. "So you're Cher Horowitz," she said. "You're very . . . vivacious."

"Thanks. It's like a creed with me," I confided. "I totally believe in the transformational potential of a positive attitude. Plus I've got this rigorous beauty regimen, but it's way satisfying and you really see results. I'd be happy to share it with you. What are you doing after school?"

"I'm co-chairing the most important charity function of the season. Thanks, anyway," Mariah said.

"Quiet everyone. Turn to your assignment," Hanratty called. "Mariah, will you do the first two equations for us?"

"I'd love to, only I can't seem to find my homework," she said, flipping through a little leather notebook that looked suspiciously like a Filofax. "Oh, Ms. Hanratty, did you get the desk set my father messengered over yesterday? He was so pleased with the A I got on Tuesday's quiz."

"It's beautiful," Hanratty fawned.

"Well, it fully should be. Those pens are Mont-

blanc—gold. Not plated. Solid gold. And so are you!"
Mariah threw Ms. Hanratty a kiss.

Instead of groaning, the whole class was smiling at
Mariah. Janet, Jesse, Amber, Sean—they were all
beaming with pride, in total kvell-overload. And Ms.
Hanratty fell for it. "Where were we?" she asked,
blushing. "All right, thank you, Mariah. Cher, will you
please do the equations?"

"Excuse me, but I was not even here yesterday," I
reminded her. "Although no one seems distraught
over that fact. And I just want to say, it is such a relief
to see how well my friends have weathered my brief
absence."

I dialed De the minute algebra was over.

"Well, I met her," I said, speaking over the noise in
the school corridor. The hallway was steeped in
changing-classes chaos.

"Who, Corey's sister?" De asked cellularly.

I spotted Baez and Ariel in the crowd coming toward
me. They waved and threw me monster smiles. We
had fully bonded in the highlands. "Her name's
Mariah, De," I said.

"Hey, Cher! Did you meet Corey Teller's sister yet?"
Ryder zoomed by, the edge of his skate narrowly
missing my pearlized designer footwear.

"Her name is Mariah," I told Ryder.

"You said that already." De sounded hurt.

"No, I was saying it to Ryder," I explained.
"Everyone's calling the poor girl 'Corey's sister.' It
must be way painful for her," I said. "It's probably no
fiesta being the sibling of TV's most desirable male
muffin."

"You are so sensitive," De cooed. "So re: Mariah. Survey says?"

I thought about it briefly. "She's rich, attractive, popular," I said, "and she so needs us. Meet you for lunch, girlfriend. Details to follow."

"It's disgusting." De greeted me at the top of the majestic steps leading down onto the Quad. "Everyone's talking about her."

As we descended, we could see the noontime crowd scattered across the manicured lawn, separating into status groups. The baked-out boardies crashed near the steep side loading ramp, which afforded them maximum skating opportunities and decent sunlight in which to read their comics. In a sandy patch known as Muscle Beach North, the jocks—male and female—were oiling up and trading fitness secrets. Brentwood brown baggers were opening their picnic hampers and unloading six packs of Maxfield private label glacier water and sun-dried tomato and basil sandwiches.

"And by her, you mean . . . ?" I asked, as we headed toward the cafeteria.

"Mariah, of course," said De. "Why, did anyone in your classes focus on anything else?"

"Well, there was minor interest in whether tattoos are protected under the First Amendment, but, no, basically Mariah was the hot topic."

"And what's disgusting, Cher, is that you were so right," De said. "They're all calling the poor girl 'Corey's sister.' "

"Tragic," I said.

We loaded up on mesclun salad and cappuccino at

the commissary and, continuing our discussion, carried our trays to our usual table in the Quad.

"Let's look at Mariah's buying habits," I proposed en route. "An Anna Sui cardigan for Tai—I mean, Anna Sui's a decent designer and all, but I'm not convinced she's in Tai's best interest. And Mariah snagged a cashmere for Amber, which is a total waste. Why even shear a goat for that? Then there's the abundant gift basket for Janet, the gold pen set for Ms. Hanratty . . ."

"Plus her brother's a total to-die-for hottie," De interrupted.

"Mariah's probably lived in his shadow all her life," I agreed. "She's probably used to people wanting things from her—"

"Like wanting to meet her brother, for instance." De set down her tray and took the Reserved sign off our table.

"How brutally demeaning," I said, "to have people falling all over you just to get close to a relative. Some people have no scruples about such things."

I was surprised that we were the first to arrive. Usually, Murray, Sean, and Jesse showed up early. And Ryder would be halfway through some processed food snack by the time they arrived. I emptied my tray, stuck it under the table, and slid in next to De.

"No scruples," De echoed disdainfully. "But it would bust fresh to get next to Corey, wouldn't it?" she added dreamily.

"Choice," I agreed. "It's always grievous not to maximize opportunity. But that's probably what people have been doing to Mariah her whole life. Sucking up to her because her father's a monster TV-producer, and her brother's a teen-soap hunk. Not that I wouldn't die to meet Corey Teller, but it's Mariah who needs us, De. Let's focus on her."

We dug into the lettuce with a hunger born of charitable intentions. "How can we aid her?" I mused.

"Well, I guess we need to help her see how humiliating and unnecessary buying affection is," De began.

"Yes, we can help her discover her own strengths, her unique beauty, what color her eyes really are. Maybe get some protein rinse into that hair before it totally withers and dies—"

"Cher, there she is. It's Mariah!"

I looked up. Mariah Teller was coming toward us. "Mariah! Over here," I called, waving her on.

"Oh, it's you," she said. "Cher, right?"

"Hi, Mariah, I'm Dionne," Dionne said. "Oh, I love that necklace. I saw it in the spring issue of *Bazaar*."

"*Vogue*," I said. "Join us, Mariah." I slid over and patted the bench beside me. "De and I were just talking about you. It's hard to be the new girl at school—"

"Not really," she said.

"We were thinking that you've got fabulous potential," De said enthusiastically.

"Potential for what?" Mariah wanted to know.

"Well, your bone structure is excellent," I said, "and I totally admire your taste in clothes—"

"You're looking at me," Mariah interrupted, "like those cosmetics counter people who do makeovers."

"Bingo!" said Dionne. "Cher lives for makeovers. It's like the thing she does best and it brings her such pleasure. I mean if there were a Michelin Guide for Makeovers, Cher would definitely get a four-star listing."

"It's how I bond, basically," I confessed.

"And if you need references," De said, "we totally redid Tai."

"Tai? Excuse me," Mariah said. "I told Tai I'd meet her at noon and I'm seriously late."

"Where are you meeting Tai?" I asked.

Mariah pointed to the far side of the patio. "Over there. My table," she said. "I'd ask you to join us, but it's usually so crowded. And you've got so much more room here."

Mariah walked away. De and I sat alone at our table. "Where is everybody?" she asked.

"Well, there's Jesse," I said, relieved.

"Have you seen Corey's sister?" he asked, without setting down his tray.

"She's on her way to her table," I said.

"Right. See you guys," said Jesse.

"Jesse, where are you going?"

"Mariah's dad and Madonna are like this," he said, crossing his fingers. "So she's going to get Madonna to autograph all of her CDs that I have."

"It's appalling how selfish some people are, how they just use other people," De said pointedly.

"Hey, I'm not selfish. This isn't just for me," Jesse argued. "She's going to sign them to Jesse *and* Arista—that's my little sister. Chronic, huh?" He left us.

Across the patio, between packed tables, striped umbrellas, and overworked busboys, Tai was weaving through lunchtime traffic. I waved to her. She gave me a classic smile, waved back enthusiastically, and hurried toward Mariah's zone.

"She'll be back," De said uncertainly.

"Never mind. Here's Murray."

"Hello, ladies," he said. "What's for lunch?"

"We're doing greens today," De said. "But the free-range chicken looked good. Bring us some sparkling water on your way back."

Murray brushed a speck off his white linen trousers. "Sorry, no can do," he said. "Mariah wants to talk series opportunities with me. Beep me later, Dionne. See you, Cher." He blew us a kiss and took off.

"I cannot believe this is happening," De said. "We are the most popular girls in this entire school, and here we are lunching alone, while Mariah's table is teeming with life."

"Dionne, comparisons are so not useful. It may look like Mariah's a magnet for relationships, but in reality everyone at that table wants something from her."

"What are you saying, that we should count our blessings because no one wants anything we have to offer?" De said, wounded.

"That is so unfair," I pointed out. "And anyway, here comes Ryder."

"Oh, great," De said, rolling her hazel eyes. "Finally, someone who wants what we have. Food."

It was true, Ryder Hubbard—baggy midcalf shorts billowing, unwashed shoulder-length hair streaming behind him—was skateboarding toward us.

"Zup, you guys? Can I like squeeze in?" Ryder said.

"Please." I gestured to the available two-thirds of our table.

"I went over to Corey Teller's sister's table, only

there's no room left. But, hey, listen, I didn't just come over here because her table's so crowded. No way. I came because she sent me."

"Mariah sent you to us?" De asked.

Ryder nodded. "She's righteously decent," he said feelingly. "Like she felt really sorry for you guys." Ryder picked a crouton out of my salad, tossed it in the air, and caught it in his mouth. "That's why she wanted me to sit with you," he explained. "So you wouldn't feel ostrich-sized."

"'Ostrich-sized'?" De looked at me.

"Ostracized," I explained.

"Whatever," Ryder said.

Chapter 8

*P*athetic is so not me. I couldn't believe anyone would think De and I needed cheering up. Or that Ryder would be the antidepressant of choice. On the way home from school, I gave the situation some serious thought. I could definitely relate to everyone's infatuation-fling with Mariah Teller. She was new, generous, and genetically well-connected, and my homies were temporarily dazzled by her. But their shabby display of enthusiasm for my and De's return reeked.

I was also slightly stung by Mariah's rebuffs. As the ultimate role models for Bronson Alcott's student body, we had reached out to Mariah. We had offered her friendship, plus a free makeover. And, incomprehensibly, she had dissed us.

Okay, and I know this is absurd. But I also had the

feeling that Mariah was purposely avoiding me. I am the least paranoid person. I mean, if someone were actually trying to hurt me I would never believe it, because hardly anyone doesn't like me.

I'm basically extremely upbeat. So it even surprised me that I was feeling wounded by the day's events. As I trudged across the floral-bordered, cobblestoned circular driveway to our front portico, I consoled myself. The way I was feeling was icky, but not like grotesquely unnatural or anything. I mean, even the most positive, popular, and attractive person can profit from a little reassurance now and then.

Mom's portrait regarded me affectionately in our entryway. I threw down my backpack and gazed up at it for a while.

"Hey, Ma, excellent day." I always put a positive spin on the things I share with her. "De and I did lunch," I said, "and for once we weren't like totally swamped by celebrity seekers and table-hopping fans. So here's my question, Ma. Do you think Daddy would feel burdened if I sought him out for a little affirmation and advice? You know how sensitive he is—"

Suddenly, Daddy's voice boomed out. "Cher, get in here!"

"Impressive, Ma. Thanks for the prompt response," I said, and hurried into Daddy's study.

"Is that shirt see-through?" Daddy barked first thing.

"Doy, it's not see-through. It's sheer. There's a difference. And I'm wearing a flesh-colored teddy underneath anyway."

He nodded distractedly.

"I'm so glad you're home, Daddy," I said. "I have this situation that I'd like to discuss with you—"

He cut me off. "Sit down, sit down. Remember last night I told you I was going to meet the most important client of my career?"

"Yes, Daddy," I said, easing into his leather-and-chrome Eames chair, which may be museum-quality but like viciously creaks.

"Well, guess who it is? You watch TV. Name me three of the top shows you watch."

"Well, the Home Shopping Network, *Ren and Stimpy*—"

"And *Coronado Cove,* right? And maybe *Sunset Beach?* And *Paradise Park?*"

"De watches all of them. She's a brutal fan," I said, picking up the little statuette of Justice that Daddy keeps on his desk. I rub it for luck sometimes. It's this lady who's blindfolded, and she's holding this balancing scale. Legend has it that Mom presented it to him after he won his first seven-figure settlement.

"And what do they all have in common?" Daddy prompted me.

"Teenagers, angst, and bikinis?" I suggested.

"Haskell Teller," he announced. "Haskell produces all of those shows, and Haskell is my new client. The reason I called you in here is that Haskell's daughter has just transferred to Bronson Alcott. Apparently, she got sick of the private academies she's gone to her whole life and decided she wanted more contact with regular kids—like you and Dionne."

"You think De and I are regular?" I protested. "As if!"

"Now, listen, Cher. I want you to go out of your way

to make the kid feel at home. Stick with her, become her best friend. It's important to me," he emphasized. "Her name is—"

"Mariah," we recited together. So much for good luck. I plunked Justice back down on Daddy's desk.

"That's her. Okay, that's it," Daddy said dismissively. "I know I can count on you, Cher. You have a real talent for making friends. You got that from your mother, I'm sure. She was a do-gooder just like you. Now, I've got some phone calls to make. I'll see you at dinner. Tell what's-her-name I want a thick, juicy steak tonight."

"Her name is Lucy, and you know red meat is terrible for you."

Daddy shook his head but grinned. "See? I told you you're a do-gooder. That's something you have in common with Haskell's daughter," he added. "She kind of runs his household, too. Her mom passed away a couple of years ago. Okay, no steak. Fish, then. Now, go, shoo, I've got a thousand things to do."

I registered the news about Mariah's mother but didn't see how it would make any difference. I mean, I already knew that Mariah and I had much in common. Popularity and high-end shopping for starters. And they hadn't proved bonding experiences.

I retrieved my backpack and went upstairs to my room. There was no way I was going to tell Daddy that I'd already tried to befriend Haskell Teller's daughter with less than satisfactory results.

I had homework to do. Fabianne, my masseuse, wasn't due for an hour yet. I considered dealing with my stress aerobically, then remembered I'd promised to send my step videos to Allison and had asked Lucy to pack them in a bubble-wrap bag and mail them for me.

Thinking of Allison reminded me of Ian. He was one of the most supportive and sensible people I'd ever met. I rifled through my bag and found his beeper number. Here was a major source for solace, I thought, and dialed the woodland hottie at once.

Waiting for Ian to call me back, I did a computer-browse. I was surfing the Internet for fashion Web sites when the phone rang. I clicked onto the Adrienne Vittadini chat room, then reached over and hit speakerphone.

"Hi, this is Ian Mallory," the warm voice of my wilderness mentor rang out. "Did someone just beep me from this number?"

"Ian, it's me, Spa Girl!" I called. "Your Leadership Award-winning pal from the true Hills of Beverly."

"Cher? Hey, great. How does it feel to be back in civilization?"

"Well, I have to say reentry's a little bumpier than I thought it would be," I confessed, tossing myself onto my bed and propping a couple of fat pillows in trippin' Laura Ashley shams behind me. "What are you doing?"

"Right now?" Ian asked. "Actually, I'm working. I'm back doing carpentry."

"And have you seen that girl you like since you got back?"

"I ran into her last night," he said. "It was so weird, I had just parked my car and was crossing the street, and there she was. I mean, she doesn't live anywhere near my neighborhood. But she just happened to be running an errand in the area."

I smiled to myself. Clueless as ever, I thought, with this kind of tender affection. It was soothing just to hear Ian's voice again, his incredible innocent enthusiasm. "Really?" I said, trying to sound as surprised as he did. "She just happened to be in the 'hood?"

"And I owe you thanks again. I mean, remember I told you how hard it was for me to talk to her? Well, I used you."

"Excuse me?"

"I couldn't think of what to say, so I just started telling her about you. You know, all the extraordinary things you did at BHNE. The rafting and rappelling rescues. How you got Allison out of her battle fatigues and into Gap classic." Ian laughed. "It was a great icebreaker. She started asking me all about you."

"And you told her I was beautiful, bright, a natural leader—thanks a lot. I don't even know the girl, and she probably hates me."

"Cher, no one could hate you," Ian said. I could feel his smile reaching through the cordless, warming me like our morning campfires.

"I know that," I said. "But sometimes, because of their own insecurity or whatever, people may not respond all that positively to someone who's into personal perfection. That's just what I wanted to talk to you about. That like happened today. There's this new girl at school. And we have lots in common. We're both attractive, popular, and generous, and are brutally responsible-type people. Only she seems furiously immune to me. It's like she has something personal against me. Only, of course, that's not even possible."

"Just give her a chance to get to know you," Ian

said. "Take my word for it, you're irresistible, Cher. Uh-oh, they're calling me. Say hi to De and the rest of the gang. Talk to you soon."

" 'Bye, Ian," I said, and he hung up.

I listened to the dial tone for a few minutes. Ian was right, I decided, getting up to click off the speakerphone. Mariah Teller didn't truly know me. Tomorrow I'd give her a real chance. I checked myself out in my three-way mirror.

What I saw there was a sincere, compassionate, attractive individual fully capable of being an excellent friend. I also noticed that the red scrunchie with which I'd tied up my hair was a shade off from my dress—but only a shallow person could dislike me for that.

Preparation is important to any endeavor. Talking to Ian had fully refreshed my faith in myself. And my massage, an hour later, was also way beneficial. Fabianne's expert fingers found the source of my tension and totally unknotted it.

"There's a clot of anxiety between your fourth and fifth chakras," she'd noted, oiling up.

"Whatever," I said, giving myself over to her shiatsu magic, which so unblocked my energy.

Doing good begins with feeling good. And, of course, feeling good begins with looking good. So I spent the rest of the evening nurturing my well-being and repairing a flawed French tip.

While I waited for the juliette on my right index finger to dry, I left-handed my computer for costume planning.

A software search for an appropriate ensemble pointed me toward a Gianni Versace four-pocket military jacket in sleek satin. With a crinoline-lace skirt and wicked urban combat boots, it would definitely set the tone for my campaign to gain Mariah's heart and mind.

I awoke early, with optimism and fabulous hair. It was loose, golden, and swished with shine and pizzazz when I swung my head. I was way glad I'd gone with squiggly rods instead of hot rollers.

I had a job to do, I reminded myself. It wasn't going to be easy, and it might not even be pleasant. But I had never let Daddy down before. So no matter how hard Mariah Teller resisted me, I was determined to win her friendship.

I didn't see her until third period. She entered Mr. Hall's class surrounded by admirers. Baez and Ariel had joined Mariah's circle, I noticed. When they came up the aisle toward me, each of them was clutching an autographed photo of Corey Teller.

"Cher, look." Ariel flashed the head shot of the grinning soap stud at me. "Isn't it jammin' that Corey's sister is in our class?"

I was going to correct her, tell her to call Mariah by her given name and not just "Corey's sister" when, unexpectedly, Mariah slipped into the seat across the aisle from me.

"Jammin'," I agreed with Ariel, and turned to face my challenge.

Mariah was wearing a choice new outfit. "I can't believe it," I cheerfully said. "I saw that Vittadini on my PC last night. It's awesome, but I didn't think it was even on the racks yet."

"It isn't. My father did the Italian shows early this week and brought it back for me," Mariah said as

Amber handed over her books and backpack. "He brought me that Versace you're wearing, too. In three different colors. But that was last year."

Amber snickered but Mariah shot her a furiously discouraging look. Then she turned back to me. "I like your hair much better today," she said, and began frantically searching through her backpack. "Let me give you the number of my guy on Beverly Boulevard. He sheared Jennifer Aniston and single-handedly created the hair of the nineties. He's pricey, but so worth it. And he might even consider doing a house call for you. I'm not sure about that. I just know he'll go anywhere for me," she said, passing me her hairdresser's card.

"Honestly, I'm totally satisfied with my stylist," I protested. "Not only does he coif, spray, cut, paint, and sculpt, he's also got a Ph.D. in psych, and you can like get counseling while your highlights take."

Mariah pressed her guy's name into my hand. "You'll thank me," she said. "And tomorrow, I'm going to bring you one of my favorite Adrienne Vittadinis——"

"Really, that's so unnecessary," I said, feeling my chakras beginning to clog up again.

Mariah ignored my protest. "It's a little knit number that I only wore once. And if you can afford it, Cher, just pick up a teensy tube of peach blush for your cheeks. Not only will it make the sweater look golden, but your whole complexion can benefit."

Remembering Daddy's request, I zipped my lip and kept smiling agreeably at her. Which Amber brutally misinterpreted.

"I'd be more than happy to advise you in the area of

my particular expertise," she offered, looking down her surgically enhanced nose at me.

"Thanks, Amber. I so need lessons on settling for less," I said.

I was spared further humiliating helpful hints by Mr. Hall, who called the class to order. "All right, today our topic is, Was the Revolutionary War truly revolutionary? Mariah Teller will do pro. Ryder Hubbard, con. Are you both ready?"

"Wow, bummer," said Ryder. "I thought we were supposed to do, Was the Civil War really civil?"

Mr. Hall didn't seem surprised. "And that is the topic you researched and prepared for us?"

"Well, I don't know about researched and prepared, but I really thought about it a lot."

"Admirable," said Mr. Hall. "And what conclusions did you reach, Ryder?"

"Well, I thought it was a pretty civil war actually for, you know, like a domestic dispute. I mean, I can definitely relate to that brother-against-brother stuff. Me and Rory get into it all the time—"

"Rory is your brother?" Mr. Hall asked.

"Yeah, and he's really spoiled, you know?" said Ryder. "One time he went on a hunger strike because I wouldn't lend him my Nine Inch Nails tape. And like my parents were all, Rory's starving, and Rory hasn't eaten in five days. And I'm thinking, two more days and he'll be too weak to stop me from snagging his Echobelly CD."

"Thank you for sharing that with us, Ryder," Mr. Hall said. "Mariah, would you like to present your arguments on why the Revolutionary War was revolutionary?"

"Oh, Mr. Hall, I was telling my father about the assignment last night," Mariah responded. "And he totally freaked. He's talking about suing the school. He says we shouldn't even be using the word *revolution* in an American classroom, much less be in favor of it. Of course, I personally have nothing against war, Mr. Hall, but he *is* my father."

Mr. Hall cleared his throat and tugged at the sleeves of his threadbare tweed jacket. "Your father talked about suing the school?" he said.

"Don't worry," Mariah urged. "I think I can keep your name out of it."

Mr. Hall nodded gratefully and moved on.

I whispered to Mariah, "You know, my father is your father's new lawyer. So if he's suing anyone, Daddy will probably be handling the case."

"Yes, my father mentioned that to me last night," said Mariah. "He suggested that we might be friends. That's why I'm being nice to you today."

My mouth flopped open and pretty much stayed that way throughout the morning. I was awed. Nothing seemed capable of stopping Mariah's generosity. She had advice on everything from lactose intolerance to shopping venues. When she pulled out her Filofax and started jotting down the digits of her favorite plastic surgeons for me, I felt things had gone too far.

Only wanting to keep my allowance, Jeep, and credit cards silenced me. Daddy has a brutally low tolerance for failure.

I was deeply grateful to lunch quietly with De. We barely glanced at Mariah's crowded table.

"She offered you a *used* sweater?" My best friend was incredulous. "Cher, that is the worst dis."

"Please," I said. "She practically foisted a makeover upon me. Could anything be more demeaning?"

"Well, we do that, don't we?" De asked. "I mean, how many girls in this very school have been saved the despair of a clueless adolescence by our gentle guidance and excellent taste?"

"Yes, but we do not foist," I pointed out. "We offer, we suggest, we urge. There's a difference," I said, spooning calorie-loaded cinnamon flecks off my cappuccino froth. "Dionne, there is way more here than meets the eye. Mariah Teller isn't just mindlessly dissing and dismissing me, it's personal. I sense bitterness here, De. And I don't understand it."

"Speaking of successful makeovers," De said, "here comes Tai."

"Hi, you guys, what's up?" Tai flopped onto the bench between us.

"Pit stop on your way to Anna Sui land?" I inquired.

"Anna Sui land? I don't get it." Tai tilted her head at me. "Oh, you mean like Mariah's table?" she said, laughing. "No, I wanted to hang with you guys. I really miss you. It's not the same over there."

"Why, did she stop buying you designer originals?" asked De.

"No, that's just it. She can't do enough for Ryder and me. Only there's like nothing she needs from us," Tai said. "You know, I told her Ryder could teach her to skate if she wanted. But she says her father's a major donor to the Olympics and he can get her like gold-medal skating instructors."

De jumped up. "There's Murray," she said. "I haven't seen him all day." She waved at him. "Murray, over here."

In his pale linen suit, Murray crossed the patio, stopping to schmooze with friends and fans along the way.

"So how'd your tap dance lesson go this morning?" De asked when he finally made it to our table.

"Whew, what a workout," he responded. "Mariah set me up with Savion Glover's coach. The man is brutal. But he says I'm coming along. I've got to stop by Mariah's table for a minute, then I'm meeting my acting teacher—"

"Will I see you after school?"

"No can do." Murray slapped his stomach. "Mariah says the TV camera adds major poundage, so I booked a session with my personal trainer before I get my head shots done. Long day. Beep me later, De."

With a friendly wave, Murray left, moving between the lunchtime tables on his way to Mariah's corner of the Quad.

De shook her head despondently.

"De, what's wrong?" Tai asked, alarmed.

"Girlfriend, we don't *do* depression," I reminded De softly. "Talk to me. Are you and Murray in crisis?"

"I don't know," Dionne confessed miserably. "He's all into Mariah and his 'career' now. Because of her, he's taking acting lessons, tap dance, voice. He's trying to shed weight for his screen test. He's shopping for an agent. He has no time left for me."

"You know, I'm kind of bummed, too," Tai said. "I really like Mariah, but I'm starting to feel like a charity case around her. She doesn't treat me like a real friend. She never hangs with me after school or borrows anything from me the way you guys do."

Dionne gave Tai a grateful little smile. But I could see

she was still hurting. "I've got an idea," I said. "It's Friday. Why don't you both come over to my house after school, and we'll plan a stress-reduction weekend of nonstop shopping?"

"Aw, that would have been so great," Tai said, disappointed, "but I already promised Ryder I'd do a movie marathon with him. There's this monster Freddy Krueger retrospective. It's like nonstop *Nightmare on Elm Street.* Don't be mad at me, okay, you guys?"

"Sure, Tai. I understand," De said. She was close to tears. "You're so lucky to have a guy like that."

"What, are you buggin'?" I said when Tai left us. "Feeling blue over Murray is one thing, Dionne; finding Ryder Hubbard alluring is totally another. Get over it, girlfriend. And anyway, we're going to have the time of our young lives this weekend. Trust me!"

Chapter 9

We were in my room, surrounded by street maps, my Thomas guide to L.A., store catalogs, recent issues of fashion mags, my *Born to Shop* Los Angeles volume, and other designer bargain guides.

"I feel better already," I told De, looking up from the collection of ads and fashion spreads I'd torn out of magazines all year. "Contemplating a spree is way relaxing."

"I've got to say I'm still a little tense," De confessed. She was flopped out on my bed. "I was just paging through this Williams-Sonoma catalog, and the kitchenware reminded me of Mariah. That girl is to relationships what a Cuisinart is to onions."

"I know," I replied, setting aside an ad for a Donna Karan outfit with hip-hugger pants that looked abdominally fabulous. "I realize this is just a temporary reprieve," I told De. "I've given Daddy my word, and I fully intend to develop a new strategy for befriending her. But I am so looking forward to a Mariah-less weekend."

"Tell me about it," said De. "So where do we start?"

We had pretty much mapped out our local options—Rodeo Drive, which does more plastic business than Amber's surgeon; Melrose Avenue, home of a fading handful of amusing vintage shops; the Pacific Design Center, where De's mom had connections to break us into showrooms usually closed to the everyday public; newly trendy Robertson Boulevard, where we planned to explore Les Habitudes and do a light munch at the Ivy; and then there was mall-o-rama, the humongous Beverly Center.

Responding to De's question, I reviewed our route aloud. "That'll take care of the morning," I said. "What are we going to do after lunch?"

"The Valley?" De suggested.

We both rolled our eyes and shouted, "As if!"

My cellular went off. "Bueno?" I said in an upbeat manner.

"Where are you?" Daddy demanded.

"I'm home," I answered. "De and I are in my room making weekend plans."

"Get down here," he ordered. "I'm in the study."

"Okay, Daddy, I'm on my way." I clicked off and turned to De. "Command performance," I said. "Check the expiration dates on all your credit cards while I'm gone, okay? It is so embarrassing when they like cut them up before your eyes."

I hurried down my side of our luxurious, wishbone-shaped staircase, which is linked at the top by a large, gracious balcony. Daddy's study is in a palatial niche tucked under the left-hand bone.

"Cancel your plans," he said as I entered the room.

"Excuse me?"

He looked up from the pile of depositions on his desk. "The Tellers are throwing a party for the cast and crew of *Coronado Cove* tomorrow. His daughter will be there, of course, and Haskell Teller specifically requested that I bring you along."

"Not even!" I blurted.

Daddy's bushy eyebrows jumped up. "I thought you'd be thrilled. What's the problem?" he asked in this challenging way.

What was I going to tell him, that I'd rather be stuck in the desert without sun block than spend a nonschool day with Mariah Teller, the girl he expected me to bond with?

"No problem," I said, struggling to keep my facial expression neutral; a smile was so not doable. For me, that is. Daddy suddenly beamed.

"Know who else Haskell invited?" he asked. "Marcia Clark."

Daddy has this adorable crush on the famous prosecutor and woman of a hundred hairdos.

"That's so decent, Daddy, the only thing is—"

He was already flipping through one of the blue-backed depositions on his desk. "Yeah?" he barked without looking up.

"Nothing. Never mind," I said. I hurried back upstairs to De.

"You look stricken," she said as I stood in the doorway.

"I am. I'm majorly bummed. Dionne, Daddy wants me to go to this bender tomorrow that Haskell Teller is throwing for the cast and crew of *Coronado Cove*. Guess who's going to be there?"

I didn't get a chance to say Mariah.

De's mouth fell open. "Corey Teller!" she screamed. She scrambled to her feet and started jumping up and down on my bed. "You're going to a party that Corey Teller is going to be at! I cannot believe it! You think this is tragic? Hello. I would give anything to be at the same party as Corey Teller!"

"Right," I said. I turned my back on De and headed back downstairs to Daddy's study.

"Can we negotiate?" I asked upon entering.

Daddy looked up. "Negotiate what?"

"My presence at this fiesta tomorrow. Daddy, my best friend, Dionne, is in crisis. She is seriously despondent because her boyfriend, Murray, is on this total career-oriented ego trip and has viciously ignored her practically all week. Now you're asking me to abandon her at this low ebb in her adolescence. Daddy, you didn't raise me to be callous—"

De must've done a gainer off my bed just then, because the ceiling over Daddy's study resounded with an ominous thud.

"What's she doing up there?" Daddy looked way concerned. "Is she trying to hurt herself? Cher, I don't think our insurance covers desperate acts committed under this roof."

"You know what would be so chronic?" I said. "If Dionne could join us at the Tellers' party. It would totally divert her from her misery. Plus wouldn't

Haskell Teller be twice as pleased if you showed up with two of his daughter's favorite classmates?"

We hammered out an agreement in under three minutes.

The Tellers' blowout was scheduled for four the following afternoon. That gave De and me a mere twenty-four hours to prepare. Doable, I decided.

I gave Daddy a big kiss, then flew back upstairs to break the good news to De.

After screaming and hugging each other, we gathered our visual aids—clippings, mags, swatches—hopped into my Jeep, and hit Via Rodeo before the shops closed down. The party was to be an afternoon affair. Dress code: informal.

For me this meant a plush Lagerfeld blue velvet minidress with excellent textured tights by Hot Sox, plus a Navajo beaded leather belt and cinnamon suede fringed boots. De did a slinky black Sonia Rykiel strapless with Cassiopeia's feather earrings. "Savage Chic" was what the *W* issue we had browsed called the look. Informal does not mean unfabulous.

We spent Saturday A.M. in a hair, nails, and skin-care frenzy. And by lift-off time, Daddy gave us the ultimate parental compliment: "You're not going out like that," he barked.

We were totally prepared for this. De and I ran upstairs, threw on the cute little cover-up sweaters we'd stashed, and hastened back to Daddy's waiting BMW.

I have lived in Beverly Hills my entire life. Wealth is my natural environment, like water and toxic waste are to a fish. I've been to multiple birthday bashes, imaginative Sweet Sixteens, astronomically expensive bar and bat mitzvahs, and countless high-ticket charity theme affairs, but until we arrived at the Tellers' fabled Malibu Canyon estate, I had never encountered a fiesta of such raw affluence.

First of all, I mistook the gatekeeper's cottage for the family quarters. The "cottage" was about the size of De's Tudor-style homestead, so it was a forgivable error. We drove through gilt-monogrammed metal gates, up a winding pebbled driveway that cut through landscaped acreage on the scale of Griffith Park. At the end of the road was the place Mariah called home—a towering restored late Renaissance castle, which we later learned had been shipped over stone by stone from Belgium. I could not even imagine the Fed Ex tab.

De and I looked at each other. "What would over-dressed be around here?" she asked.

"You tell me," I said. "This place puts my allowance in bleak perspective."

A fleet of valets was helping guests from their cars. De and I stepped out, and while Daddy shook a few hands in the driveway, we tossed our sweaters into the backseat of the Beemer.

The party was set up in a tented village behind the main house. It had the festive feel of a Cirque du Soleil event: the colorful striped tents, the glittering costumes, the dazzled spectators not knowing which exciting act to focus on first. Paparazzi roamed the grounds. *Extra* and *ET* camera crews stalked celebrities. Three different groups provided the sounds—a classical string quartet, a jazz trio, and a major dance DJ who used to mix melodies at the Viper—while four bowling-alley-length buffet tables handled refreshments.

I lost Daddy in the first five minutes and De a short while later. Separated from my homies and in search of low-cal hors d'oeuvres, I drifted toward one of the buffets. Its centerpiece was an ice sculpture of the *Coronado Cove* crest. I was loading up on grapes and admiring this work of art when another guest jostled my arm. "Excuse me," we both said. Then I looked up, stunned.

"Cher?" It was Ian. He was all dressed up. Well, his jeans were ironed, anyway. Plus he was wearing a proper tie and vintage corduroy jacket with his traditional flannel shirt. He looked Baldwinian as ever, but more so.

"This is so fresh! I can't believe it," I said, immediately hugging his hunky frame. "Ian! What are you doing here?"

"I work on the show," he said with that fabulous grin that lit up the entire fruit and cheese section of the buffet. "I'm with the crew, building and repairing sets. I told you I was doing carpentry, remember?"

"Yes, but you didn't say *Coronado Cove!* That's way impressive."

Still grinning, he shrugged his classic shoulders. "If you really want to be impressed, let me give you a tour of this place."

"Excellent," I said.

We ambled out into the sunny afternoon, and Ian explained about how Haskell Teller had fallen in love with the castle in Europe and had it mailed home and restored. Ian pointed out things like the Belgian granite tiles on a terrace bordered with citrus trees and flowers, and the way sandstone and oak had been used to accent the mullioned windows with their adorable little leaded panes.

"How do you know all this?" I asked as we meandered toward the stables, tennis courts, and pool area.

"Architecture major, remember?" He pointed out a fabulous artificial lake on the property. It was surrounded by acres of gardens and orchards created, Ian explained, by the same man who had redesigned part of a famous Paris park called the Tuileries Gardens. "It's hard to recapture a seventeenth-century feel with twentieth-century materials," he said.

"Totally," I agreed.

Ian laughed. "You're bored, right? What you really want is to meet some of the Coronado Covies."

"You are so wrong," I insisted. "Outside of shopping, I like live for culture."

"Well, there's plenty of it here," he said as we circled back to the big top.

"De and I did a lap when we arrived," I told him, "but the only cast member we even saw was Andy Duncan, who's got these monster freckles and is way skinnier than you'd think. We never spotted Scott Morrison, my personal fave, or even Corey Teller. Is he as def in real life as he is on the tube?"

"'Def'?" Ian asked, scanning the crowd. "I'm not sure, but— Okay, there he is. That's Corey over there. See," he said, pointing. "He's with that gorgeous girl in the black dress."

I launched myself onto my toes, but I couldn't see through the circle of frantic photographers surrounding Corey and the girl. Hospitably, Ian lifted me up.

I sighted Corey Teller posing against a tent pole. A brutal babe in a ravishing Rykiel was looking up at him. From what I could see, Corey was as outstandingly blond and beautiful as his publicity shots, and much taller than I'd imagined. The girl barely came up to his famous square jaw. She was slender, dark, and . . . Dionne!

"Ian, it's Del" I shrieked excitedly, "That gorgeous girl Corey's with is Dionne!" I was furiously happy for my homie. "Okay, thanks. You can put me down now."

Ian lowered me to the ground. And suddenly I was face-to-face with Mariah. She was making the rounds with Andy, the spotted Covie.

"Hi," I said. "Way festive blowout."

Andy Duncan gave me a nimble smile. "Hey," he said, Hollywood-style, "nice to see you," and wandered off.

"Oh, hi," Mariah returned my greeting with zero enthusiasm. The unexpected sight of me at her gathering was obviously not the highlight of her afternoon.

"Ian's been showing me around your compound," I gushed, trying to pump some positive energy into the moment. "Oh, this is my friend Ian."

"I know," she said, bloodlessly pale. "He works for my father."

Mariah was poured into a hot red Oscar de la Renta that did excellent things for her classic face and ice blond hair.

Ian must have felt the awkward vibe between us. He gallantly came to my rescue. "That's a . . . nice dress . . . um, er . . ."

"Mariah," I whispered.

"Mariah," he said, with his most alluring grin.

"Thank you," the zombie who'd eaten Mariah replied.

All of a sudden I saw Daddy heading in our direction. He'd spotted me with Haskell's daughter, and he was all smiles.

"Mariah," I began desperately, "I so love this amazing casa. Ian was filling me in on it. Our place is kind of cute, too. Why don't you let me reciprocate for this chronic bash, and come for brunch tomorrow, say two-ish?"

Mariah looked at me like I was speaking English as a second language. I realized that a visit to our estate was not going to wow the girl. Still, it wasn't like I'd invited her to tour urban decay. And Daddy was upon us now.

"I'm afraid I'm busy," she said, and turning on her lizard strap Manolos, she left us.

"Was that Teller's kid?" Daddy asked.

"Isn't she cute?" I said. "I was just introducing her to my friend Ian. Daddy, Ian was one of our guides at BHNE."

Ian extended one of his callused palms and shook Daddy's hand. "Nice to meet you," he said.

Daddy winced and retrieved his hand. "What are you, a lumberjack?" he asked suspiciously.

"Well, I do work with wood."

"Ian's studying to be an architect, Daddy," I said. "And he—"

"Hey, is that Marcia Clark over there with Haskell?" Daddy asked suddenly. "I think it is. Good luck in your career," he said distractedly to Ian. "And remember, there are more things you can make with lumber than with spotted owls, any day."

"Daddy can be so adorable. He's majorly infatuated with Marcia Clark. So the other night, you said you owed me," I reminded Ian. "It's payback time. I need someone to dance with."

"I'm not all that good," he protested.

"Well, I am, and if I can raft and rappel, you can reggae." I took Ian's hand, and we cut through the crowd to the dance floor. The music raged, and soon Ian and I were lost in action.

All of a sudden flashbulbs started popping. "Cher!" I heard De call to me. She was dancing with Corey. A mass of photographers and camera people swirled around them.

I waved to her. "Look who I found—Ian!"

"How dope! Ian, hi!" De was waving at us.

Then, for a second, I got totally spooked. I thought I felt someone watching me. I looked and there was Mariah at the edge of the dance floor. She'd been gazing at me, or at least in my direction. She looked tall, slim, striking, yet she seemed fully dismal.

It was hard to believe my presence could make anyone so unhappy. Maybe it was because her brother was always surrounded by people that she seemed so forlorn. I didn't get much beyond that; Mariah acknowledged me with a cold smile and vanished back into the crowd.

"Ian Mallory, just the guy I'm looking for," a familiar husky voice said. I turned and found myself staring into a pair of piercing blue eyes.

"Scott," Ian said. "Hey, I was wondering where you were."

Scott Morrison, who played *Coronado Cove's* bad boy, Jake Thatchet, broke eye contact with me momentarily to greet Ian.

"Yeah, I've been looking for you, too," he said. "Frantic bash. What a palace, huh?"

"Well, a castle, anyway." Ian laughed. "Scott, this is Cher. She's a fan of yours."

Like who wouldn't be, I thought. Here was this astounding guy with dark, nearly black, choppy-cut hair and excellent rough-hewn features—a fighter's nose, fabulous Native American style cheekbones and complexion, plus those amazing full lips that could, and often did, totally fill the small screen in mouth-to-mouth close-ups.

Scott Morrison's raging blue eyes locked back onto mine with a nearly audible click. "The feeling is totally mutual," he said in that great scratchy voice. "I noticed you about an hour ago, then you disappeared."

"Ian and I did this tour of the grounds," I said. "He's a down guide. Architecturally excellent."

"Oh, I know all about Mallory," Scott said. "You're the one I want to find out more about."

"You sound exactly like Jake!" I said with this little laugh. I mean, on *Coronado Cove* Jake is a total evil girl-trap, and here he was eyeing me with that sleepy Thatchet gaze.

"He wishes. If Scott got tangled up in half the action Jake gets into, he'd be too wiped out to show up at this party," Ian said, grinning. "Don't be fooled. He's much nicer than Jake, Cher, and he can dance better, too."

"Nice?" Scott said. "A two-bedroom condo in Silicon Valley is *nice*. I am . . . an hombre, man. And, yes, an excellent dancer." He held out his arms for me.

"Ian, do you mind?" I asked.

"No, please, dance." With a gracious gesture, he backed away from us. "Catch you two later."

Scott and I started moving to the music when, all of a sudden, some of the cameras that had been focused on De and Corey swung our way. Voices called, "Scott, Scott, over here, Scott!" And I was dancing blind, with dozens of black dots exploding over Scott's smiling face.

Finally, he grabbed my hand. "Thanks, thanks," he said to the photographers, and he led me off the floor. "Let's get out of here. Why don't you give me that tour Ian gave you?" he suggested.

"As soon as I can focus again," I promised. "Does this happen to you all the time?"

"Meeting someone like you?" He did his Jake Thatchet thing again. "Not ever."

We walked down toward the lake. There was this clean breeze rippling the surface of the water. Everything was softer, quieter, even our laughter as we talked. I told Scott how Ian and I had met and pointed out some of the things he'd shown me. And I found out that Scott was nineteen, but he'd been an actor for practically ever. Then he started talking about his two years on *Coronado Cove*.

"It's weird. I mean, I hardly know sometimes where Jake ends and I begin," he said. "Ian's been a really good buddy. He's so . . . normal, I guess. You know, most girls find Ian much easier to be with than me. When they look at me, they see Jake."

"I know," I said. "And they must feel like they already know you, right? I mean, I do. And I don't . . . know you, I mean."

"But so far?"

"What, like how excellent are you? You are a serious hottie in your own right," I said, laughing. "Uh-oh, see that person up there on the hill waving at us?"

"The father type?" Scott said.

"Totally. That's Daddy. Guess we're going."

We started back to the party. "Listen, I'm going house hunting in Santa Barbara next Saturday," Scott said. "Ian's coming along, in his capacity as architectural guru, to check out sites and buildings. Why don't you come with us?"

"Sounds excellent," I said. "But I've got to check with Daddy."

When we got back to the party, Ian was standing near Daddy. "Scott just invited me to go to Santa Barbara next weekend," I announced.

"I hope you said yes," Ian said. "It's going to be a great trip."

"Who's Scott?" Daddy demanded.

I introduced them. "He works for Haskell Teller," I added. "Can I go, Daddy?"

"With two boys I've never laid eyes on before?"

"Bring along a friend." Ian jumped to the rescue again.

"If you do, she'll be sitting in the back with Ian," Scott quietly assured me.

"What a great idea. Ian, you know that babe you like, why don't you invite her?" I suggested.

He shook his head. "I can't. She'd never go with me."

"I can't believe you. That is so negative," I remarked. "Do you even know how perfect it would be? I mean, you already told her about me. So then she'd get a chance to see—"

"What, that you're *not* a bright, beautiful, natural-born leader?" Ian teased. "I can't do it yet, Cher. I still get tongue-tied around her. But that doesn't mean you can't bring a friend along. Maybe De would like to come."

"Where is Dionne?" Daddy said. "It's getting late."

"Just follow the flashbulbs," I told him.

We went in search of De. Ian and Scott tagged along. We found her near the chamber music quartet. Corey Teller was jotting down De's beeper number as we approached.

"Cher, Ian, hey!" she said.

Dionne was furiously aglow, way infatuated. And I have to say that she and Corey made an attractive couple, yet didn't quite earn that special click I get when viewing a perfect match. Plus the thought of their pairdom evoked a wince of guilty compassion in me for Murray.

"Everyone knows Corey, right?" De asked.

Ian nodded. Scott laughed, and slipped his arm around my waist. I said, "Nice meeting you, and thanks for this excellent bash."

"My dad pulled it together. With Mariah's help, of course," Corey added, as the brutally blond-capped, red de la Renta pulled up beside him.

Mariah's faux green eyes did a quick survey of our little group. I saw them bounce from Scott to me and back. She took in the arm circling my waist. Then, startlingly, Mariah's sad yet sullen glare dissolved, and she threw me a full-out smile.

Hello, was that happy gleam actually aimed at me, I marveled. What was up with the teen soap heiress? Had I been a blond cadet about the girl? Could Mariah's recent cold behavior and moody glances actually have been so not personal?

I am usually way intuitive. But I was willing to embrace the possibility that I'd been wrong. I returned her pleased expression and snuggled closer to Scott.

"Mariah does all of Dad's parties, and mine, too. We'd be lost without her," Corey said as Mariah inclined her head modestly. "Dad calls her the power behind the throne, right?"

"I'm the anonymous Teller," she said playfully.

"Not at our school, you're not," De responded. "Mariah's taken Bronson Alcott totally by storm."

"Well, that was the idea, wasn't it?" Corey laughed. "Every princess needs a kingdom of her own."

And a prince, I thought. Which was so weird. I mean, I hadn't even wondered whether Mariah had a special someone in her life. Whenever I'd seen her at the party she'd been pretty much alone. Except for that one time with skinny, freckled Andy Duncan. Now my heart quickened. What a find Mariah Teller would be for some lucky Baldwin.

Then I had this vicious brainstorm.

"Excuse us," I said, and pulled Daddy away from the others. "What if Mariah Teller came to Santa Barbara with us, Daddy?" I asked. "Then could I go?"

He gave me a little interested smile. Then he glanced over at Ian and Scott. He looked as if he was going to ask them to put their hands on the buffet table so he could pat them down for weapons. Daddy is so protective. I mean, he spends his life in court defending barons of industry and commerce, so he's fully aware of society's lowest elements.

Finally he said, "If Haskell Teller goes along with it, I'll give it serious thought. There'll be conditions, of course."

"Of course, Daddy," I said. "I'm totally prepared to negotiate."

I gave him a vicious hug, then hurried back over to De and company. I grabbed her arm. "We've really got to go," I said, smiling at everyone. "Mariah, thanks so much for having us here. You're sure you can't stop by tomorrow? Lucy does an excellent brunch."

It was just a shot in the dark. I knew she'd turn me down.

"Tomorrow's impossible," Mariah said. "Really. But let's do lunch on Monday."

"Monday," I echoed, surprised, but smiling for Daddy's sake. "Excellent. Your table or mine?"

"Let's do yours. It's so much quieter," she said.

Chapter 10

We made the news! There was tons of local coverage on the *Coronado Cove* bender. Footage of De and Corey showed up on Sunday's eleven o'clock weekend roundup, and there was a shot of Scott and me dancing on MTV News.

Everyone was all over me the next day at school. A beaming Tai accosted me in the parking lot. "You are so famous! Why didn't you let me know? I would've taped you guys!"

"Can you even believe it?" I said. "I mean it was only like a video moment, but I thought my dress looked classic."

"And so velvet," said Tai as we moved toward the Quad. "Plus I really have to say that Scott Morrison is even hotter on MTV than he is on regular TV. You two look so excellent together."

My cell phone went off. "Hang on, I've got a call coming in."

"That's okay. Catch you later," she said, giving me a giant hug that painfully dug the silver baby beads on my necklace into my clavicle. "I'm meeting Mariah for croissants and latte at the bean bar—but she didn't make MTV!" Tai reminded me, then ran off.

I clicked my mobile. It was De. "Girlfriend, I know you caught the news!" she cried.

"Dionne, you have total star quality!" I said excitedly. "Tai saw me and Scott on MTV!"

Ringo Farbstein, the math whiz who dated Janet Hong, gave me a high-five and mouthed, "Way to go." I nodded thanks.

"Frantic," said De. "And know what else? We made the weekend party page of the L.A. Times."

"Both of us?" I asked

Alana and Baez were hurrying toward me. I smiled at them, then signaled that I was on the phone. They nodded their heads, indicating that they understood my predicament.

"I don't know," De said as I watched Alana and Baez scribbling me a note. "The picture kind of focuses on me and Corey, but you might be in the background. It's hard to tell."

"Where are you?"

Baez tore the note out of Alana's loose-leaf binder and handed it to me, then they left.

"I'm trying to make my way through the cafeteria crush," De said. "So many kids have been stopping me that Sean and Jesse are like playing bodyguards."

"Tell me about it," I said, opening the folded scrap of loose-leaf paper: "Is Scott Morrison as hot as Jake

Thatchet?" Alana wanted to know. Baez had added, "And in what ways? Be specific!"

"De, I'll call you later," I said, tucking the questionnaire into the pocket of my petite leather mini. "Someone's on my other line." I hit the button.

"Cher, it's me, Summer. I'm home with the hives. Turn on MTV! Turn on MTV!"

"I can't. I'm at school. Are they rerunning it?" I screamed.

Neil Jeffrey, this puffed-up tennis jock, crossed my path just then and threw me this smoldering gaze.

"Never mind. It's over," Summer said. "There was this girl who looks exactly like you who was dancing with, you know, Scott Morrison from *Coronado Cove?*"

"Summer, that *was* me!"

"Get out."

"It was!" I cried, grateful that Neil had moved on. He might be the hunk of the senior class, but he was so high school. "I was at this celeb-studded blowout at Mariah's, and there were all these TV people there. Oh, and guess who else? Ian Mallory from BHNE. He said to say hi!"

"I'm plotzing. I'm calling Ariel right now."

She was gone. As I tucked my cellular into my fuzzy pink bear backpack, a shadow fell across my path. Glancing up, I saw Amber blocking the sun. She was wearing a colorful knit garment with these little chenille spheres all over it. She looked like the Velcro backdrop of a Nerf ball tossing game.

"You're not going to Amanda Goodman's bat mitzvah, are you?" she demanded. "Because I was thinking about wearing a blue velvet dress similar to the one you wore to Mariah's party—"

"How do you know what I wore to Mariah's party?"

"I talk to her every day," Amber said with a touch of indignation. "I mean, I haven't talked to her today . . . yet. But I do keep up with media events."

"You mean you saw me on MTV, right?"

"Oh, I wouldn't go that far. I was just channel surfing and the dress caught my eye."

I saw Dionne heading up the marble steps, flanked by Sean and Jesse. "Well, I'm not wearing it to your cousin's bat mitzvah. I don't even know your cousin. Thanks for checking in, Amber," I said, and called to De.

"So like what are Scott's favorite disks?" Jesse asked as I joined them on the steps. "Is he really into Springsteen, like they say in the trades? I don't know, he looks more Morrissey to me."

"He hasn't confided his musical preferences," I said. "Will you excuse us now? De and I need a bonding moment."

"Thanks, Sean. Thanks, Jesse. I don't know what I would have done without you." De blew them parting kisses. She looked totally fresh in this teeny T and triple-sheer layered skirt. Actually she looked a lot like Olivia, who played Corey's love interest on the *Cove*. "What a morning," she said as her honor guard disappeared through the doors ahead of us. "I couldn't go anywhere without kids doggin' me for personal stats on Corey and the other Covies."

"I know. It's like déjà vu, isn't it?" I said, nodding to this group of girls who were standing at the head of the stairs, beaming at us.

"Things are way back to normal," De agreed. "We

are once again the most sought-after Bettys at Bronson Alcott High."

We paused to autograph the scraps of paper the girls thrust at us, then passed through the bronze doors they held open.

"Exactly," I commented as we moved along the corridor to our classes. "Only different."

This awed Barney in droopy jeans with last year's Calvins showing at the waistband handed De a fabric pen and asked her to sign his Abba T-shirt. "What do you mean?" De asked me.

"I'm not saying that I don't cherish my return to raging popularity," I tried to explain. "I'm totally comfortable with being idolized. But something doesn't feel right. You know how everyone wants something from Mariah?"

"Absolutely," De agreed. "I mean, if it isn't some high-ticket designer trinket, it's Corey's autograph or, as with Murray, a cameo on one of her father's TV shows—"

"Well, now I want something from her, too. I want her to go to Santa Barbara with me next Saturday, so that I can be with Scott."

"And?"

"It isn't right, Dionne. Not unless I have something to offer her in return. And as you know, Mariah has already rebuffed the free yet fabulous makeover we subtly proposed. What else is there? I mean, I've racked my brain—"

"Girlfriend," De gasped, "are you saying you're willing to sacrifice a once-in-a-lifetime romance op for principles?"

"Not even!" I assured her. "But there's something

icky about all this." The bell rang. "Well, thanks for listening," I said.

"Do you feel better?" De asked.

"Unburdened, maybe. But not actually good." We did a limp-wristed Beverly Hills high-five. Then I ducked into algebra.

It was there, as Ms. Hanratty chalked mind-numbing equations on the board, that I began to understand what was wrong.

As Dionne had said, we were once again the undis-puted, most sought-after Bettys at Bronson Alcott High. We could barely take a step without kids throw-ing themselves at us, groveling for inside info on Corey or Scott. Of course, I was thrilled to be in popular demand again. But, I realized with a jolt, I preferred to be sought-after because of who I was—not because of who I knew.

"Cher?" Ms. Hanratty called.

"Present."

"I realize that. Can you tell us what x equals in this equation?" She was tapping the blackboard.

I had totally not been paying attention. "Well, it seems to me," I began, "that if you consider the relationship between x and, say, y and—what's that squiggly next to y?"

"That 'squiggly' is called pi," Ms. Hanratty said as if she had a personal stake in it; as if pi was like this guy she was dating or something and I'd just called him a Barney.

Mariah was sitting across the aisle. "Forty-eight," she whispered. "Take my word for it. Janet checked my homework."

"Oh, well," I said, "then x has to be forty-eight."

"Good. Now, Amber," said Hanratty.

I turned to Mariah. "Thanks," I whispered. "I was lost in thought."

She gave me this little emerald-eyed wink. "I'm so looking forward to lunch," she said.

Our reserved table in the Quad was beginning to fill. While De and I waited for Mariah and picked at our grilled mahi mahi, Jesse, Janet, Ariel, and Sean had drifted over and set down their trays.

"He looked like an excellent dancer," Ariel was saying with this hushed kind of reverence.

"He is," De and I answered simultaneously.

"Who?" Jesse asked.

"Oh, I meant Scott Morrison," said Ariel. "After Summer called me, I had my Watchman tuned to MTV all morning. Sorry, De, I didn't catch you and Corey on the tube last night. But Sondra showed me the *L.A. Times* clip. Fabulous coverage. Was that a Sonia Rykiel cinching you?"

"Wasn't that shot of Corey and me classic?" De responded. "Oh, and guess who else we met at the bash? Ian!"

Ariel shrieked. "Ian Mallory, who like saved me from drowning practically?"

"Isn't he the best?" I said. "Although I think I deserve a little credit for the rescue—"

"Isn't who the best?" Mariah had arrived with Amber and a train of worshippers in tow.

"Ian. You know, the guy I was talking to at the party. Here, scooch in." I made room for Mariah between De and me.

"What about me? Like what do I look like?" Amber foolishly demanded. She was carrying two trays, her own and Mariah's.

Alana checked out Amber's multicolored, striped ensemble. "An awning at the Psychedelic Café?" she guessed.

Sean zoned in on the chenille balls. "Joseph's Technicolor Zit Coat?"

"Cher and I need a moment. I'll meet you all over there," Mariah said to her fans, indicating her usual table at the far end of the patio. "We'll do dessert."

Amber looked sullen. Not exactly a new look for her. Yet she had no choice but to set down Mariah's sushi platter and split.

"You were talking about Ian?" A flicker of confused concern crossed Mariah's pale face. "Then Scott's not the one you're interested in?"

"Ian is a fan and a friend," I explained. "But Scott is Baldwin to the max. A monster hottie. Viciously decent."

Was that enormous relief I sensed in Mariah's sigh? "Don't you agree?" I asked.

"I've known Scott for ages," said Mariah, removing her chopsticks from their paper wrapper. "I just don't think of him that way. But the two of you looked awesome together. Much better than you looked with Ian. I mean," she said, reddening furiously, "Ian's too . . ."

"Flannel?" De suggested.

I kicked her under the table. The plan here was to ignite Mariah's interest in Ian, not highlight his fashion flaws.

"Ow!" Dionne barked. "Er . . . so you've known Scott for ages?" De gave me this frantically apologetic look, then tried again to engage Mariah in conversation. "I guess you've known Corey for quite a while, too?" she said.

"All my life."

"Oh, right," said De. "Like you'd probably know whether he's dating anyone special?"

"He broke up with Cheryl Anders of *Sunset Beach* two weeks ago."

"Cheryl Anders! She is so def. So then Corey is probably all pining and grieving, right?" De sounded worried. "Like he's probably ripe for a rebound."

"Corey doesn't do pine," Mariah said. "A month ago he split with Jennifer Younger—"

"Jennifer Younger of *Paradise Park?*" Sean was suddenly involved. "So, she's like free now?"

"Right." Ariel rolled her eyes. "All five-feet-eleven furiously toned inches of Jennifer Younger are free— and brutally starved for a high-school hip-hop boy in a sideways baseball cap. Doy, I don't think so, Sean."

"So he plays the field, is that what you're saying?" De pursued her quiz on Corey's availability.

"Would you say Scott is kind of free and easy with his affection as well?" I probed.

"No. Scott's t.b. But Ian must have masses of romantically inclined admirers. Would you say that?" asked Mariah.

"There was this one girl, Sydney, at BHNE, who practically threw herself off a cliff to get his attention," Ariel contributed. "But Ian's way foggy in his girl-sighting skills, right, Cher?"

"Really?" Mariah's prawn-bearing chopsticks paused in their flight to her lips. She turned to me. "Sounds like you're like the ultimate authority on Ian Mallory. So is he interested in anyone?"

This was the test.

I knew Ian had his shy but stunning eye on some lucky babe—the Betty who'd bumped into him accidentally on purpose the night he'd returned from BHNE. The one he couldn't get up the nerve to invite to Santa Barbara. So the answer to Mariah's question was yes. Ian Mallory was interested in someone.

But if I told Mariah that, then why would she want to go to Santa Barbara with him? I didn't see Mariah as a romance-wrecker type. Or someone who'd settle for second-best. And if Mariah didn't go to Santa Barbara, chances were Daddy would squash the trip.

Suddenly I knew what Daddy's petite statuette of Justice must've felt like. Small, blind, and just sitting there with this set of flimsy scales, trying to balance out what was fair.

My cellular rang. "Excuse me, please," I said, way relieved. I pulled the phone out of my backpack. "Bueno?"

"Cher, it's me," Murray said. "Don't say my name. I've got to talk to you. I'm two tables behind you guys."

I craned my neck trying to see him.

"Yo, yo, yo! No, stop, don't look over at me! Don't tell Dionne that you're talking to me. She's looking over here!" He hung up.

Perplexed, I stared at my cellular.

"Who was that?" De asked.

"A random breather," I responded.

"Eeeww. Grossissimo."

"Corey gets calls like that all the time," said Mariah.

"Not even!" De squealed. "How heinous."

"Well, I've really got to run," I said, getting up quickly.

"Cher, wait." It was Mariah. "Um . . . so I was wondering . . . You know that makeover you offered me?"

I nodded, speechless.

"Is the offer still good?" she asked.

"Yes," I said. "It's still good."

"Well, I'd consider it a great favor," Mariah Teller said.

Dionne cheered. "You won't regret this, Mariah. Your hair will thank you."

"Cher is the best," Ariel said supportively. "She changed my life with two words—matte finish."

"That is so excellent, Mariah," I replied. "And a furious coincidence—because I've got this favor to ask of you, too. Are you free after school today?"

Mariah paged through her Filofax, and I clicked on my electronic organizer.

"I've got a four-o'clock with my father's nutritionist; and then it's facial and massage," she said. "Delia goes postal if I even think of skipping. She says, 'Life is maintenance.' Tomorrow?"

"What wisdom," I agreed. "Oops. Tomorrow Tony, my personal trainer, is leading the step class at S.E.T.S. I promised I'd show up to support him. How's Wednesday?" I was getting nervous now. I really wanted to nail down a private moment with Mariah before the weekend. And I wanted to seriously contribute to her life before requesting anything of her.

"I can't believe it," she said, sounding genuinely annoyed. "This entire week is booked."

"I so understand," I consoled, struggling with my own feelings. "It's difficult to be in demand." I switched off my organizer. "Well, next week then?"

Mariah brightened suddenly. "What about Saturday?"

"Saturday?" I could feel De staring at me. Are you really going to give up a once-in-a-lifetime romance op for principles? she had asked earlier. I knew that question would still be in her eyes. "Let me get back to you on that," I suggested. "Let's talk later. I've really got to run."

I left the table without even glancing at Dionne and hurried to Ms. Geist's social studies class. It took me nearly ten minutes to get there. Every few feet, someone would stop me either to tell me how great I looked on MTV or to ask for vital stats on Scott. In class, I could barely concentrate. Five different kids sent me notes. Also, although I found myself jotting down Scott's initials in various interesting scripts, I was starting to get sick of hearing other people talk about him.

I glanced out the window. Murray was standing there, frantically signaling to me. A school security officer was coming up behind him. Our security people wear these fabulous little black uniforms that go with everything. Before I could figure out exactly what was happening, this guard grabbed Murray and hauled him away.

It was the same story in Mr. Hall's class. Everyone was asking me about Scott. Kids sent me notes. And then Murray crashed the class.

"Hey, Mr. Hall, how's it going?" he said, picking a piece of lint off the sleeve of his navy blazer.

"Just fine, Murray. I think everything's under control," Mr. Hall replied. "What can I do for you?"

"Well, actually, I need to speak with Cher Horowitz. Er, my guidance counselor suggested I . . . Well, you know, Mr. Hall, that Cher's father is a famous lawyer and I . . . um . . . need representation. Yeah. Ah . . . due to a minor infraction of school rules. And . . . I'm sure Cher is as fine a legal mind as Bronson Alcott offers. So I wondered if you'd please excuse her—and also, since this involves preparing my case, if you'd keep it confidential that I stopped by. You know, the client-lawyer relationship is kind of sacred. So . . . um . . . Cher—" Murray held his hand out for me. "If you'd just . . . I really need to discuss my case with you. Now." He turned back to Mr. Hall. "Is that all right with you?"

"Please," said Mr. Hall. "In fact, I insist. Cher, would you be good enough to accompany Murray so that the rest of us can get back to the business at hand?"

"But I was so enthralled with Amber's heroic defense of catalog shopping, Mr. Hall," I said. "Where would we be without J. Crew, Eddie Bauer, L.L. Bean, Victoria's Secret, oh, and Garnett Hall, which uses like totally natural fibers? Are you sure it's okay for me to go?"

"Trust me," he said, nodding his adorable bald head.

I packed up my books and accepted the class's applause. Then Murray and I exited.

"You know I'll do my best to help you," I told him as we headed down the nearly deserted hallway toward the bronze doors.

"I knew I could count on you," he said. "So what's Corey Teller really like? You met him, right? Is he really as tall as he looked in that picture in the *Times?* Is he taller than me?" Murray asked. "What about his teeth, are they real? See—" Murray flashed me a big smile full of braces. "Mine are. Is the guy a phony?"

"I can't believe you yanked me out of class just to further your *Coronado Cove* ambitions, Murray," I said indignantly. "My education means nothing to you. All you care about is fishing for information to help your career."

"And I can't believe you would accuse me of something so self-serving." He held the door open for me, and we emerged, blinking, into the sunlight. "I'm bruised by your unsubstantiated charges. Furiously hurt, Cher. I'm not doing this for myself," he insisted as we descended the marble steps to the Quad.

"Right," I said sarcastically. "Do you have any idea how tiring it is to be like this living authority on *Cove* trivia? People at this school seem to have forgotten who I am. All they care about is what I know about Corey Teller and Scott Morrison. What about me? What about Cher Horowitz?"

"I care, Cher," Murray said. "I care about you, and I care about De. That's why I'm trying to find out what kind of guy Corey Teller really is. I saw that picture in the Sunday paper. I saw the way De was looking at him. I've got to tell you, Cher, Corey's got this grave reputation as a serial dater. He's got a new woman every week. Frankly, I'm concerned because I think De's falling for him and I just don't want the girl getting hurt. What's that noise?"

"My cellular," I said.

"If it's De, don't say anything, okay? About me talking to you. Uh-oh!"

"What's wrong?" I asked, but, following Murray's anxious gaze, I saw one of our elegantly garbed guards tearing across the Quad toward us.

"I'm Audi," Murray shouted, disappearing through a stand of stately palm trees.

I took the call. It was Mariah. "I've been thinking," she said. "I could blow off my riding lesson tomorrow. And how about if I get the cast of *Paradise Park* to sign up for that step class with your personal trainer? Would that be supportive enough? Then we could like get together after school and map out my renovation."

"The entire cast?" I said excitedly. "Tony will totally gloat. Girlfriend, this is so doable."

Chapter 11

*E*very successful makeover begins with planning. I spent several hours in cordless consultation Monday evening with Dionne. "Okay, we're in agreement on the moisturizing protein-rich conditioner, lose the lenses, tone down the lipstick thing," she said. "But I still think you should invite her to Santa Barbara first thing. Just to get it over with."

"De, everyone we know wants something from Mariah. I am in the unique position of having something to offer her. I'm not going to barge in and burden her with my needs."

"She seemed pretty positive on Ian at lunch, didn't she?"

"It was way heartening. But that presents its own problems. I mean, Ian's already in like with someone—who, of course, may not be half as worthy or adorable as Mariah. Still, one has to respect his taste. So what do you think about Gucci for daywear?"

"Making a comeback," De decided.

The next day, as Mariah's driver whisked me toward the Tellers' castle, De and I maintained cellular contact. "Okay, read me the list again," she urged.

" 'Make her feel at ease,' " I recited. "Mariah should be way more comfortable in her own home."

"That's not a home, it's a planet," De interjected. "Next?"

" 'Check out her fitness regimen.' We already know she has a stable, tennis courts, a nutritionist on retainer, plus full exercise facilities at home. But I thought we'd do some sports to test endurance, hand-eye coordination, muscle tone, general prowess. I was thinking tennis."

"Excellent. I bet she could get Agassi and Brooke over for doubles."

I moved on. " 'Culture quiz. See what she's into,' " I said. "If necessary, I'll call in Jesse to see if her CD collection's up to date."

"Cher, I have to say, I basically approve the way she dresses," Dionne remarked. "Solid labels. Interesting mix of designers—classical as well as contemporary, with some progressive next-wave artists included."

"I agree. But five-figure jewelry for school days seems excessive. I don't think she needs a brutal couture overhaul, just a little toning down."

"That's it. Sounds like you're ready," De confirmed. "Don't forget to pry into Corey's feelings for me, okay?"

I'd promised her last night that I would. Now I asked

cautiously, "Dionne, would you be crushed if Corey Teller wasn't, you know, a totally sincere type of person?"

"He's not," De said matter-of-factly. "Didn't you hear Mariah reel off his recent conquests? I mean, girlfriend, don't you read the tabloids or monitor *Inside Edition* or *Hard Copy*? Just find out if he intends to phone me. I'm not looking for commitment, just something to get Murray's attention."

I couldn't tell De she had more than that already. I had, after all, promised Murray confidentiality. "Will do," I said. "Okay, I see the gates ahead. Wish me luck, girlfriend."

"You go, girl. Don't forget, I'll be standing by."

Mariah's housekeeper directed me to the bungalow beside the tennis courts where, she said, I'd be able to change. I followed her directions down the tiled, floral-bordered path. Mariah was already on the clay, practic-ing her serve with a way decent-looking, long-haired pro. He had this red bandanna tied around his richly tanned forehead, and he was wearing this striking white shorts set. It was an excellent athletic look.

Mariah was in tennis whites, too. Her long legs were well-muscled, her arms slender and strong. Basically, she was fully toned. And seemed to have a choice serve.

Good, I thought. I wouldn't have to introduce Mariah to the wonders of stretching and aerobics the way I'd had to do with Tai.

I waved to her on my way to the bungalow. She gave me this big smile and called, "I'll be right there. Grab an iced tea or whatever. Okay, Rod," she told her pro.

"Daddy wants half an hour at the net tomorrow, and Corey's got to cancel. Rebook him for Friday, seven A.M. See you Thursday."

He did this little bow, gave me a gleaming smile, and started collecting tennis balls as Mariah left the court.

"Do you really want to play?" she asked me, coming over. "I was just warming up with Rod, but really, I'd much rather just hang and chat."

"That's dope. My business here is done," I told her candidly. "The idea was to explore your athletic aptitude and evaluate your toning and shaping needs. You're in majorly prime condition."

"Thanks," she said, tossing a towel around her neck and flopping down into a courtside chair.

I sat beside her. "So you book tennis time for your father and brother?"

"They're so dependent when it comes to health and fitness needs."

"Tell me about it. I just finished doing Daddy's dental and periodontal schedule for the next quarter; plus then I had to input all the appointments on his computer and set the reminder alarm on his organizer. Why are males so incompetent?"

"That totally resonates," Mariah said. "Since my mother died, my father and brother are just helpless."

"I know. My mom died about a million years ago," I confided. "But I have to say, last year Daddy actually booked a flight for himself and picked out a dozen shirts all alone at Barneys. He didn't even use a personal shopper. And I only had to return two of them! It gets easier," I promised her. "Of course, I only have one man to take care of. You have two."

Mariah got up and tossed her towel onto her chair. "Corey's not so bad. He's just forgetful," she said, stretching. "And so busy."

"So I heard," I commented, remembering her brother's industrial-strength dating schedule.

"The girl thing, right?" Mariah extended her hand to me and pulled me up.

"The girl thing," I confirmed. "Corey's got a rep as America's most wanted muffin."

We started walking back toward the house together. It was a quiet afternoon, and the extravagant floral arrangements of the Teller gardens were arrayed in blazing Technicolor.

"Poor Corey," Mariah said. "He can't look at someone without it making headlines. The media makes such a fuss about how he's got a new girl every week, but really they sort of started the whole thing. They had Corey appearing on these 'eligible bachelor' lists practically before he had his driving permit."

"He's fully licensed now." I laughed. "You're right, though. The press is way attracted to him. I mean they totally swarmed him and De at the *Cove* bash. Viewing that thirty seconds of local news coverage, you'd never have guessed that Corey and Dionne had just met. It looked like they were a solid item. At least that's the way it looked to Murray."

"Is that good or bad?" Mariah wanted to know.

"Useful," I decided. "Murray's been neglecting her. He got way involved in career issues. But when he saw the shot of Corey and De in the paper, he woke up to the possible high price of fame. And speaking of fame, having such a high-profile sib must be way exhausting. I mean, De and I just got our pictures taken with Corey and Scott and like that's all people have been focusing on."

"You get used to it." Mariah shrugged. "I mean, Corey is extremely talented, popular, naturally gorgeous, and a major international attraction. My mother was, too. It's natural for people to be curious about them. And everyone knows my father, of course. He's just this brilliant taste-maker and TV producer who like totally knows what today's youth wants—"

"Right. Babes in bikinis." We both laughed.

"You've got the best smile," Mariah said suddenly. "Who do you use for laminates? Daddy, Corey, and I get ours done in New York. Oh, and I got this amazing Alaïa at Bloomie's last time I was there. You know Alaïa, don't you?"

"I live for Alaïa," I said.

"Well, I got this outstanding Alaïa sweater that turned out to be totally the wrong shade for me and I've never even worn it and really, Cher, you've just got to take it. It'll be so perfect with your incredible blue eyes."

I stopped in my tracks. "Mariah," I said, "can I ask you something? Why are you always giving people things?"

Those too-green eyes scanned my face as if I had the answer. "Well," Mariah said after a moment, "because I have so much. I mean, look around. I live in a castle."

"Does Corey give clothes away, too?" I asked.

"Corey? Of course not, he doesn't have to," she said too quickly. "I mean, everyone loves Corey—"

"Right, and the feeling is so mutual," I blurted.

"What?" Mariah blinked at me, then she started to

laugh. "Oh, you mean Corey loves everyone. It does kind of look that way. But, really, he's—"

"Corey aside," I said, getting back on track, "I just have to say that giving has to be balanced by accepting the gifts of others. Otherwise, it like tilts the scales in a brutally uneven manner. Your accepting my makeover offer is an excellent start. And, by the way, your smile is chronic, too," I said. "Excellent laminates."

"Thanks," Mariah said, and we started toward the house again.

"Is De furiously attracted to Corey?" she asked. "I mean, would she feel burned if he moved on?"

"Dionne is realistic and way resilient," I assured her. "She'll be fine if Murray does the right thing—which he definitely will."

"With your help, right?" We were at the back terrace with its imported granite tiles, and these cute lemon trees in bleached wooden tubs, and like noble works of sculpture all over the place.

"I have a certain talent in the romance arena," I confessed. "I can usually spot a choice match before the couple involved can. Something just goes click. It's this gift. And I'd have to say I didn't actually get the click on Corey and De. But what about you? Is there a Baldwin in your picture?"

Mariah ducked her head. Her bleached strands bobbed fetchingly. "There's someone I feel a certain way about," she said, almost shyly. "And I just have this feeling that he really likes me, too. Only I don't know how to be . . ."

"How to be what?" I pressed.

"Anything." Mariah gave me this smile. "I mean, you know, anything but Corey Teller's little sister or the daughter of *Paradise Park, Coronado Cove,* and *Sunset Beach.*" We were at her back door. She paused with a hand on this ancient iron door handle. "I think if one more person asks me one more question about Corey or my father's shows, I'll totally spew."

"Girlfriend, De and I have had just two days of reflected glory, and I can brutally relate."

Mariah opened the creaking back door, and we entered this cavernous kitchen. Rainbows of light poured through stained glass windows, glancing off an awesome collection of copper pots that hung over an enormous old worktable. The whitewashed walls were lined with thick wooden shelves filled with fabulous European crockery. And the long worktable held mounds of fresh fruit and a huge pitcher of new-cut flowers.

"I'm way sick of having my brother's fame and my father's fortune impress people," Mariah confided, as we stood beneath the kitchen's Gothic arch. She did this little laugh. "As **if** that's all that makes me special."

"As if I" I echoed.

She flashed this confident grin, which lasted about as long as a diet at a sleepover. "I mean, I'm bright, popular, and attractive. But, face it, I'm not as talented as Corey. I'm not as smart as my Dad. And I'm not as beautiful as my mother was. So sometimes it's like, what am I? Who am I?" She tried to smile again, but she wasn't having much luck with it. "Cher, I furiously want to be my own person—but where do I begin?"

I was momentarily startled. We were talking more than a surface makeover here. And although I brutally wanted to inspect Mariah's all-star wardrobe, her poignant confession called for a change of plans.

"Where else?" I said. "At the mall. Get changed. I'll call De and have her meet us. Then we're Audi!"

We boutique-hopped, paid plastic, and escalated tier to tier through the middle-income spending arenas of L.A. The point, as I told Dionne when I phone-prepped her for the foray, was not to acquire elite merchandise but to give Mariah a feel for basic mall-mania. Something fast, fun, and friendly. A democratic rather than designer experience. I wanted to remove Mariah as far as possible from the competitive fabulousness of her native milieu.

What better place to end our tour of plebeian pleasures than the food court. Which was where the three of us were, surrounded by shopping bags and pigging on grease-soaked curly fries and cheese-drenched nachos, when Mariah flipped De and me totally out.

"Well," De was saying, frantically forgetting Mariah's relationship to the boy in question, "it's day four, nearly eight P.M., and no call from Corey. Could this mean our brief fling is over?"

"Possible," I guessed. "Murray will be so pleased. I'm not at liberty to divulge details, De, but you know he really cares."

"I know," she said, grinning. "But I was hoping a little drama might drive him to bold, new demonstrations of affection. Murray is so not romantic. I mean, the last time he sent me flowers was before our first date."

"What kind?" I asked.

"Roses," De said, licking a string of melted cheddar from the corner of her lips. "A full, fall-down fabulous dozen long-stemmed yellow roses. And, girlfriend, they smelled so sweet. Even Carolina was impressed."

"That's De's mom," I told Mariah. "It takes quite a bit to impress her." I napkined my fry-greased fingers and tore a nacho from the cheesed clump.

"Long-stemmed roses. I love that," Mariah said, knocking back a fry.

"Yes, and they were the final flowers. The only ones he ever sent. Plus, the boy never remembers what I like or don't like. A gift from Murray is like a box of chocolates."

"I think that's sweet," Mariah protested. "He buys you chocolates."

"No," De explained. "I meant, you never know what you'll get. I was like paraphrasing *Forrest Gump*."

Mariah nodded and separated another curly fry from its paper nest.

"Friday is our anniversary," De continued. "I just hope Murray got sufficiently torn up over the Corey episode to at least remember our occasion. I can't stand to admit this, but I kind of miss his adorable ghetto garb and urban argot. It's been too long since he called me 'woman.' "

"Scott beeped me yesterday to find out if Daddy had said yes yet about—" I glanced at Mariah, who was waiting for me to continue.

"Mariah," I said, hoping to divert her, "isn't this noble, the three of us sucking up curly cuts together? I'm so glad you decided to have lunch with me on Monday. I was kind of shocked because I actually entertained the notion that you might not like me. And I usually don't do insecure."

Dionne choked on a nacho chip. "Hot sauce," she rasped in explanation, but I knew she thought I'd been too candid.

I hadn't meant to blurt out my suspicions. I'd just wanted to avoid the Santa Barbara issue. But now that I'd begun, I just kind of marched forward, mouth first. "Was it my imagination or was there something awkward standing between us earlier in the relationship?"

"Well, yeah, I guess," Mariah said, suddenly squirmy.

De shook her head at me, then turned compassionately to Mariah. "Cher sensed it," she said. "You were like totally not falling all over her the way everyone else always does, and it so bruised her ego. She's way more vulnerable than she lets on."

"Thank you, Dionne. You can dispense with the memorial service, I'm actually here in person. Why?" I asked Mariah. "Was I insensitive or callous in some majorly random way?"

"Not really. It wasn't your fault at all."

I glared triumphantly at De.

"I really owe you an apology, Cher," Mariah said. "It was all this tragic case of mistaken identity. The minute I saw you with Scott, I knew how wrong I'd been. I was just jealous. The boy I like was at the bash, and I thought you and he were—" Mariah shrugged.

The guy she liked had been at the *Cove* fiesta. Which boy, I wondered. I did a ten-second replay of party events.

Andy Duncan, the freckled Covie, was the only guy

I'd seen her with. But I'd only exchanged about two words with him. Plus while he'd seemed nice and all, I'd never have picked him as a match for Mariah. There was no accounting for taste, I reminded myself.

"Well, I'm totally relieved that you saw my gleam for Scott and discounted me as competition," I told Mariah. "Now, let's focus on your guy-getting strategy—"

"Well, so far, it's not producing much in the way of results," Mariah confessed. "I mean, the biggest, boldest thing I've done to try to get his attention was to show up practically on his doorstep one night. And all he said was, 'What are you doing in this neighborhood?' I mean, he was totally psyched to see me. I could tell that much. His face lit up. And what a gorgeous face it is—"

There was something way familiar about this tale. Hello, I didn't need Janet Hong to help me with the equation. Suddenly, everything fell into place. "And that gorgeous face was freckle-free?" I probed.

Mariah laughed. "He doesn't have freckles."

"So, this night, when you accosted him on his home turf, then he started to tell you about this girl he met, right?" I said gently.

De's juliettes paused above the nacho heap. She gave me this look. "What are you talking about?"

"That's right." Mariah laughed. "He usually has such a hard time talking to me, and all of a sudden he was way eloquent—and it was all about this other girl he'd met."

"How painful," De said dramatically.

"And bitterly confusing. Because it was the most

animated conversation we'd ever had—and it was all about Cher."

"Cher?" Dionne was lost. "Your man was telling you all about Cher?"

"Mariah!" I leaped up, lunged across the table, and gave her a bone-crunching hug. "You're the Betty Ian's wild for! Go, girl! He told me all about it."

"Ian?" Dionne asked.

"That's why you were so cold. I knew it!"

Mariah held me at arm's length. "Did you say he's wild for me? Did Ian tell you that?"

"Ian Mallory?" De was still coming to grips with reality.

"Yes, girlfriend, he did," I told Mariah. "I am so totally blown away by this excellent occurence. You and Ian are a definite click."

"So where do we go from here?" Mariah asked.

"Santa Barbara," I said.

My beeper went off. I checked the number. Murray was paging me from his car phone. "Excuse me." I grabbed a final curly fry and pushed back from the table. "Mariah, why don't you connect the dots for De; fill her in on the Ian scene. I'll be right back," I promised. And, sucking down the fry, I left them at the food court. I needed a secluded venue from which to return Murray's 911.

Chapter 12

On Friday evening, I was so excited I thought I'd hurl. I get that way before an important makeover. My perfectionist issue seriously surfaces.

Dionne was no help. "Aren't you psyched?" she kept saying. "This is possibly the most significant renovation of your career. Mariah is so high profile. And her father is your dad's biggest client."

I bit my tongue and eyed De sympathetically. Normally, I might have snapped on her, but today was Dionne and Murray's anniversary, and I knew that he had not as yet acknowleged it.

Mariah's limo would cruise into our circular driveway at any moment, delivering my new friend and formidable client for what we all hoped would be a spectacular sleepover-makeover experience. And it had to be right the first time around. We were leaving early in the morning for Santa Barbara. There'd be no turning back if the protein rinse bit.

Scott and Ian were totally prepped for the outing. When I broke the news to the Mallory-man that Mariah was going to join us, he had a moment of ecstasy followed by raw panic. "I won't be able to talk to her," Ian said.

"I've got it handled," I assured him, and told him about the article I was faxing him on Ten Classic Conversation Starters. "Of course, I tinkered with the recommendations," I admitted. "Like the one about 'If you were a fruit, what would you be?' I changed it to 'If you were a house . . .' You know, to take advantage of your architectural expertise. Trust me, Ian. You'll be fine."

I didn't tell him about the *YM* piece I'd faxed to Mariah on how to get your guy to gush. In it, six hotties reveal why they clam up when it's time to open up. I mean, this article showed that even hunks like *YM's* celeb of the month, Antonio Sabato Jr., have a hard time talking about feelings.

I knew we were ready. I'd had Mariah's color chart done. And in addition to the downscale mall duds I'd helped her select, I had pulled an array of possible outfits from my own revolving closet racks. Plus I'd arranged a scientific assortment of FDA-approved products on the cute skirted table in my dressing room.

My assistants, Dionne and Amber, were suited up and ready. We'd decided to go with a Banana Republic look for the transformation. So we were in like cuffed khakis and cap-sleeved pique shirts with petite pearlized buttons. Predictably, Amber had added a lace bolero to her ensemble. I let it go. I didn't want to be rigid or anything.

My cellular rang. I clicked it on. Daddy said, "Haskell Teller's limo just pulled in."

"Be right there, Daddy," I chirped. "And thanks again for saying I could go tomorrow. You are so sweet."

"You're welcome—and don't forget, you girls are to stay in cellular contact or Haskell will send out the helicopters. He's got two pilots on call. Now, get down here."

"I'll be right there, Daddy," I said, heading for the door. "Mariah's here, I'm going down to get her," I informed De and Amber.

De looked up from the color chart she was reviewing. "You know this entire chart is bogus until we find out what's under those emerald lenses."

"Thank you for sharing," I said, and went downstairs to greet Mariah. She'd brought only two suitcases and a backpack with her for the sleepover. It was an impressive display of trust. It told me that she knew I'd have everything else she needed.

Mariah's actual eyes turned out to be radically stunning. Unadorned, they were this pale, cat green shade with golden flecks. So De was right. Our color chart was practically useless now. We abandoned our original hair plan and went with a gold-hued conditioning rinse that softened Mariah's entire look and perfectly accessorized those spectacular eyes. And yes, Mariah had brought along the clear contact lenses I'd suggested she pack.

"What drew you to emerald green?" I asked as Amber applied a protein replenisher to Mariah's bleach-bombed follicles.

"I was sort of going for an over-the-top look," she confessed.

"I totally get that," De sympathized. "It's that Madonna, Drew B., Courtney Love thing. A cosmetic cry for notoriety."

Mariah shot her a look.

"Or whatever," De demurred.

"Also, my mother's eyes were brilliantly green," she added.

"My mom's were blue. Much bluer than mine," I said.

"Okay, Mariah, time to rinse," Amber said, wiping her hands on the monogrammed Calvin Klein bath sheet I'd tossed over Mariah's shoulders.

As Amber led Mariah to the shower, the phone rang. I glanced at my new Breitling Chronomat watch, which combined aesthetic excellence and outstanding technical performance. Murray was right on time. I hit speakerphone. "Hello, who is it?" I asked.

"Yo, yo, Cher. I been looking all over for Dionne," said Murray. "She be there? Send her down. I got to see my woman—now!"

De whirled toward the phone. Then she looked up at me. This monster smile broke out. "Murray?" she whispered.

I nodded.

"Oh, right," she said to the speakerphone, "like he never even acknowledged that today's our anniversary, and now I'm supposed to think he's dope 'cause he tracked me to your casa and wants a word with me? Not even!" she said.

"Yo, yo, is that my woman?" said Murray.

"Don't call me woman!" said De.

I glanced out the window. Cell phone to his ear, Murray was sitting in his BMW convertible, which was parked in our driveway, not too far from the picture window in Daddy's study. Gone was the deconstructed linen look. Murray was back in basic Hilfiger and Rasta wear—with this black knit cap pulled low over his locks.

"Go downstairs," I ordered De, "before Daddy gets involved."

It was too late. My cellular rang. "Hello, Daddy," I said. "It's just Murray. Yes, he does look just like one of those people on TV. You mean like on MTV, right? Oh, you meant Court TV. Well, that, too, I guess. Dionne's coming right down. Yes, the same Murray De's always gone out with."

"Go!" I told Dionne. She checked her makeup and smoothed down the nipped-in waist of her cute little pique blouse.

"He called me woman," she said. "I'm totally kvelling."

The moment De left, I rushed to the speakerphone. "She's on her way. Did you pick up the chocolate truffles?"

"Excuse me?" said Murray. "You didn't say nothing 'bout chocolate."

"Hello, I said truffles. Little round, rich and creamy Godiva chocolates—and you got what?"

"Er, potato chips," Murray said sheepishly. "I, er, thought you said Ruffles."

I sighed deeply. "Did you at least get the flowers?"

"Yellow roses, just like the ones I got her before our first date. A full dozen, long stemmed and sweet smelling. Can you see me from the window?"

I looked down. "I can see your hat. Isn't wool a bit warm?" I asked.

Murray looked up at me and flashed me a big, gold-capped grin. Then he tore off his cap. His dreads were gone. "Can you read it?" he asked.

Dionne was shaved into his scalp. "Chronic touch," I applauded. "Way imaginative. Two thumbs up, Murray."

De emerged from under our front portico just then, hands on her hips, ready to debate.

I hung up and gave them their moment. My cell phone rang again. "Haskell's on the phone," Daddy said. "He wants to speak to Mariah. He can't remember where he left his blood pressure pills."

"She's in the shower now. But tell him to look in the kitchen, Daddy. On the windowsill over the sink, or next to the fruit bowl on the table. That's where I keep yours."

"Okay, hang on," he said. I carried my mobile to the window and watched De and Murray bonding once more in blissful confrontation. Then Daddy was back on the line.

"Okay, his pills were on the kitchen table," Daddy said gratefully.

"Excellent," I said.

"But that doesn't mean I won't order out the helicopters if you two break phone contact tomorrow. Don't forget, you've got to check in every two hours." There was a pause. "Know what Haskell said when he found his pills? 'Mel, you're a genius,'" Daddy reminisced proudly. "Haskell Teller called me a genius."

"And you are, Daddy," I said.

Chapter 13

*T*he sky was cloudless and the exact color of Scott's chronic blue eyes. The ocean was equally awesome. As glittering as a Versace bustier, it glinted with these sequinlike reflections of the sun. The temp was balmy; not so hot and humid that it would frizz your 'do, yet sunny enough to make wearing Web shades more than a status statement. It was your traditional California-type day—minus earthquakes, mudslides, and smog alerts.

We soared coastally toward Santa Barbara. I was buckled up beside Scott in the front seat of his rec vehicle: a squat, wide Hummer, the total military-looking car most likely to be valet-parked at L.A.'s power eateries.

Mariah, her new honey gold locks alive with body

and shine, was bouncing along in the backseat with Ian. We'd done her up in trendy workwear—fabulous generic-looking khakis and a vintage faded flannel shirt, which furiously set off her gold-flecked eyes.

I could tell that Ian and Mariah had both done their homework. Silence was so not happening between them. Laughter and some excellent excerpts would float forward, and every now and then I'd hear familiar phrases like "Have you ever cried in front of a girl?" and "Which famous person, living or dead, would you most like to meet and why?"

Outside of like Martin Luther King, John Kennedy—father or son, actually—and like either Donna Karan or Calvin Klein, my answer to that question would have been Scott Morrison. And here I was whizzing up the Pacific Coast Highway with the raspy-voiced bad boy of prime time himself.

Scott had been filling me in on the specs of his dream home. He wanted privacy, but not isolation; a small-town feel with big-city convenience, and though he loved the beach, he thought he'd like to live in the mountains. So Ian had suggested he check out Santa Barbara, which was a mere ninety miles from downtown L.A.

Then I launched into my BHNE field and stream adventure, and how Ian had helped us overcome my severe home-decorating difficulties. Scott was furiously amused. "So then we threw this pajama party in this totally haunted hovel with a wildlife-friendly latrine and like coyotes barking in the backyard. And we tried to get it catered by some of L.A.'s most celebrated bistros, who brutally refused to deliver," I was saying when my watch alarm went off.

"Oops. Check-in time."

"Good girl," Scott said as I dialed Daddy. "Don't want Mel and Haskell's airborne squad swooping down on us."

"Hi, Daddy. We're still on the road," I reported.

"Where exactly?" He was so cute. He'd mounted a map in his study and had these little pins in it representing Mariah and me. He was charting the progress of our journey.

"Well, we're way past Oxnard. And I can see like an oil rig out on the ocean. And I think we're not that far from Santa Barbara."

"Okay. Got you. Check back at four."

I hung up and reset my Breitling.

"There it is ahead." Ian leaned forward. "Let's head up to Montecito. There are some extraordinary places hidden along those winding roads."

We climbed toward the stars, literally. The homes tucked away in what they called Upper Village belonged to some of Hollywood's major audio-visual personas. There'd been Heather Locklear, Keanu Reeves, and Christian Slater sightings; and elderly hotties such as John Travolta and Steven Seagal were sometimes among the local attractions.

As we cruised, Ian did his tour-guide thing.

Santa Barbara had been discovered in the 1500s by two different guys, both of them Spanish, who traveled up from Mexico. One came by sea and one came by land. The seaman, Juan Cabrillo, found the Chumash Indians, who lived in the area from Malibu through San Luis Obispo. In fact, Ian informed us, Malibu was a

Chumash word. He didn't know what it meant, but I wouldn't be surprised if it was like Native American for totally golden or brutally choice.

The guy who came by land was like this monk called Padre Junipero Serra. He walked. I mean, majorly. He founded twenty-one missions from San Diego to San Francisco, an awesome stroll even today. And the one in Santa Barbara was called the Queen of the Missions.

And the Queen had this fully excellent shopping facility a couple of miles away in a mall called Paseo Nuevo, which featured brand-name shops as well as adorable local boutiques arrayed along an avenue of brick walkways just nine blocks from the Pacific.

As our Hummer headed into Montecito, it became evident that there were major spending opportunities in the hills, as well. We paused for frozen yogurt at an elegant bistro on the main drag where prices were totally up to Beverly Hills standards and everyone was wearing these chic baseball caps with major designer tags. And it was all like the less famous the celebrity, the bigger the sunglasses.

I'm not naming names, but Scott and Ian ran into this guy who'd been on exactly two episodes of ER and one segment of *Coronado Cove*. And he had on this backward baseball cap plus a pair of aviator shades that obscured two-thirds of his so not recognizable face. It was like, oh yes, I'd know that chin anywhere.

The faux celeb introduced us to a real estate person named Fritzie, whose sun specs recalled Darth Vader's helmet. In her Cherokee, license plate REEL ESTATE— as in *reels* of film, indicating that Fritzie's clientele was motion-picture related—she led us along Coast Village Road, where our house-hunting expedition kicked into high gear.

Amazing casas were sprinkled throughout the area, each sparking its own romantic fantasy. There was the sprawling mountain-top ranch with its piñon wood beams, chestnut plank floors, giant stone fireplaces, and massive leather sofas.

Fritzie was way inspired by the place. "So masculine, so abundant," she declared.

"So what do you think?" Scott asked me as we traipsed from room to awesome room.

"It's not you," I ventured.

"Why not?" Mariah asked.

"I don't know, the size is all wrong," I said.

"You mean the dimensions?" Ian was grinning. I could see he agreed with me.

"I guess," I said. "It's like one of those vintage double-breasted Armanis. I mean, this place is all shoulder pads. It totally drapes around your ankles. But I love the location."

And I did. I could definitely imagine Scott and me on horseback, riding side by side along the crest of the hill, overlooking the quaint town and sparkling ocean.

We viewed a faux English manor, its gatehouse guarded by two regal lions carved in stone. It was like this discount version of Mariah's castle. But I could picture picnics bordered by formal gardens and candlelight pizza pig-outs amidst the fragrant eucalyptus trees.

Fritzie also had the keys to the mansion of a muscular superstar. In addition to a fully stocked gym, including a regulation-size boxing ring that Ian and

Scott couldn't resist trying out, the high-tech sports complex boasted outdoor and indoor pools, both with hot tubs.

"Can you just see us lounging in designer terry cloth on the tanning deck?" I asked Mariah. "You know, like nursing wheat grass juice and living the good life?"

"It's not the warmest home I've ever seen," she said dryly.

I totally agreed. "Please," I said, "this place is like a rehab for the aerobically challenged."

We did a few more rustically casual, high-ticket cabins laden with every modern convenience. Then we left Fritzie and cruised down toward town. Sea level at last, we wandered through the mission, which was probably the most beautiful property we'd seen all day, then hit Paseo Nuevo for a rejuvenating spending spree.

At four my trusty watch chirped, and I placed a call to Daddy. "We're going to get a bite before we head home," I told him. I gave him our coordinates—"Nine hundred block of State Street"—sent love, and hung up. "Where are we going to eat?" I asked.

"Excellent question," Mariah said. "Shopping so depletes me. I'm up for a major carbo refuel."

So then we were all, "How about Italian? We could do Palezzio's in Montecito." We were following the red brick road, walking aimlessly toward the water. "Or Kai for Japanese has a nice rep. And there's Acacia, which does California grill—"

Ian kept exercising his veto, shaking his head. "I'm in beautiful people overload," he said. "I need some-place basic and real."

We were down near the wharf. Seagulls were soaring

over the ocean. The sky was cloudless. The sand was clean. "Now, that's basic and real," I murmured, staring out at the sea.

Scott took my hand. Ian put his arm around Mariah's shoulder, and she curled up against him. The four of us stood there quietly for a while, feeling the sea breeze hash our hair.

"I've got a def idea," Ian said after a while.

"Def?" Scott shot him this amused look.

"Def. That's right, Cher, isn't it?" Ian asked. "Doesn't it mean excellent? Like jammin', fresh, dope, doable?"

Mariah burst out laughing. We all did.

"No, no, really," Ian said through his own laughter. "Here's the plan. Cher and I will make dinner."

I stopped laughing. "Excuse me?"

"She's a terrific wilderness cook. Come on, Cher," Ian encouraged me. "We'll find a quiet beach, fish, forage, do a campfire—"

"Jump off a cliff, shoot the rapids in a rubber raft, do a five-mile hike in new shoes, dip into an icy lake at five A.M.—" I recited sarcastically, at first. But then I started to recall the entire experience and got this warm, gooey glow.

"Can you really do all that?" Scott asked in that raw Baldwin whisper of his. "And cook, too?"

"Can you start a fire?" I asked him.

"I hope so," he said. "I mean, how am I doing so far?"

I laughed. "Not that kind of fire."

It was nearly sunset. We were the only people on this secluded stretch of beach. We'd parked on the bluffs and hiked down through narrow, winding roads and lush greenery to this perfect strip of sand.

We'd messed around for a while, racing along the water's edge, tossing the Frisbee Scott had unearthed from the back of the Hummer, playing tag football. We were like this total diet soft-drink commercial for being young, beautiful, and athletically correct. And then Mariah and I had flopped down onto the sand, and Ian and Scott decided to start collecting wood for the campfire.

"I think he really likes me," Mariah confided, staring all dewy eyed at Ian's retreating, plaid-clad back.

"Definitely," I agreed. "And what's even more nimble is that Ian seems to know you like him, too. That's a furious leap forward for the boy, trust me."

"Cher," Mariah's commanding voice became small. Between the sea breeze and the lapping surf, I could hardly hear her. "This is just the total best day," she said.

Then she got kind of squirmy. "How can I thank you?" Mariah said, twisting her ring, beginning to ease it off her pinky.

I put my hands on hers and stopped her. "You mean, aside from giving me something?" I asked.

She looked down at our entwined hands, then up at me. "I'd really like to——" she began. Then she shook her head and started over in this stronger, more familiar Mariah-type voice. "Cher, do you know how hard it is for me to just accept how excellent you've been? You know, like without trying to repay you for it?"

"Mariah," I said, "do you know how hard it is for me to pass up a Cartier trinket?" I laughed, but I was way proud of the girl. "Anyway," I pointed out, "I couldn't have done this trip without you. Daddy wouldn't have let me go. So we're totally even."

Mariah's grin widened to a sparkling, fully laminated smile. "So you think Ian really likes me, right? Scott is clearly drawn to you. Which is so not difficult to understand. Even at the party, he said, 'Your friend is a frantic babe.' My friend, that's what he called you," she said. Then, she added, "Are you?"

"I don't know." I pretended to think about it for a sec. Then I said, "What'll you give me if I say yes?"

Mariah blinked at me, then she cracked up. And we started splashing sand at each other and were like furiously laughing and screaming. And Ian and Scott heard us shrieking and came like Rescue 911. Which just seemed so whack and, for some reason, made us laugh even harder. So there we were, Mariah and me, so extravagantly hysterical that we could hardly catch our breath.

Now, in the early twilight, the shells and scraps of our fish and clam feast were scattered around us in the sand. Mariah was finishing up the greens she and Ian had foraged. The campfire Scott had made was leaping orange, red, and blue into the purpling sky.

Ian pulled Mariah to her feet. "Let's go down to the water," he said. Sitting in the sand, Scott and I watched them walk to the ocean's edge.

"Excellent day," Scott said after a while.

"Frantically fresh," I concurred.

"Only one thing missing," he decided. "Dessert."

"We could look for berries?" I offered.

Scott shook his head. "Not sweet enough," he said. Then he took my face in his warm, sandy hands and

I saw those famous lips in close up, just before they touched my own.

My heart began to frantically beat. In fact, it was thudding so furiously that when Scott pulled away and shouted, "What is that!" I thought for a minute that he'd meant my heart.

"Oh, no!" he yelled above this deafening pounding. "Cher, you forgot to call your father, didn't you?"

Suddenly a sandstorm swirled around us. We looked up to see two helicopters circling above. Then a bullhorn bellowed, "Cher, answer the phone!"

Fumbling wildly, I pulled my cellular out of my backpack. "Hi, Daddy," I said. "I couldn't hear it ringing with all that noise. You must have a choice view from up there. Isn't Santa Barbara totally classic?"

"Are you all right?" Daddy demanded. "Is that Mariah down there near the water?"

As if she'd heard him, Mariah looked up and waved.

"We're both brutally fine, Daddy. Is Haskell with you?"

"He's in the other helicopter. Hold on, the pilot says he wants to talk to me." I held. Mariah turned to me and started to laugh.

I tried to stay serious. Daddy was back. "Okay. That was Haskell. He says to ask Mariah to reschedule his shiatsu massage for tomorrow. And I want you home no later than nine. We're going back now. Haskell's giving a dinner party for Marcia Clark tonight. And, Cher—"

"Yes, Daddy?" I asked.

"Which tie should I wear with my new jacket, the Lanvin or the Gucci?"

"Not even!" I gasped. "Marcia is furiously American,

Daddy. She's like a total national treasure. It's got to be Calvin or Ralph.''

Mariah and Ian ran through the wind and sand back to our campfire. Then I broke cellular contact, and the four of us stood on the beach and waved as the helicopters veered off into the setting sun.

About the Author

H. B. Gilmour is the author of the best-selling novelizations *Clueless*™ and *Pretty in Pink*, as well as *Clueless*™: *Achieving Personal Perfection*; *Clueless*™: *Cher's Guide to . . . Whatever*; *Clarissa Explains It All: Boys*; the well-reviewed young-adult novel *Ask Me If I Care*; and more than fifteen other books for adults and young people.